Defence in Depth

D1586247

Defence in Depth

Martin Hoffman

faber and faber

LONDON · BOSTON

First published in 1985
by Faber and Faber Limited
3 Queen Square London WC1N 3AU

Filmset by Wilmaset Birkenhead Merseyside
Printed in Great Britain by
Butler and Tanner Ltd Frome Somerset
All rights reserved

British Library Cataloguing in Publication Data

Hoffman, Martin
Defence in depth.
1. Contract bridge—Defensive play
I. Title
795.41'53   GV1282.42
ISBN 0–571–13527–7
ISBN 0–571–13531–5 Pbk

Library of Congress Cataloging in Publication Data applied for.

Contents

PART II: DEALS 32–65

Foreword

Broadly speaking, there are three different skills in bridge: bidding, declarer's play, defensive play. Almost everyone would agree that the order of difficulty was: defence, by far; dummy play; bidding.

Anyone with average card sense can learn to bid reasonably and to play the dummy fairly well. Defence seems to be more a matter of natural talent and experience. But most players do not develop such skill as they may possess.

The problems in this book are divided, quite roughly, into two sections, of which the first is somewhat easier than the second. Even so, unless you are already a very competent performer, you won't get many of the answers right at first – and if you do, you may not be sure of the reason and you may feel that you would probably have done the wrong thing at the table. Don't worry about that – so would most players. But in time you will find that you have learned to think along the right lines.

While technical ability is important, it is not everything by any means. Here, if you like to think of it in that way, are Ten Commandments for the defending side:

1. Listen to the bidding. This means, don't just hear what is said, but attempt to construct the hands of all the players. You will be surprised at the number of inferences you can draw if you really try.

2. Questions during the bidding? There are four possible courses of action. Ask no questions at all; ask only at the end of the bidding; ask at every turn when opponents are playing a complicated system; ask only when a bid is made which you do not wholly understand. Most players follow this last course. This is the worst because if you ask, for example, what three spades means, you are telling the world that the bid has some interest for you. Two possibilities then arise: the opponents may form an opinion about your spade holding; and partner may do the same, thus running the risk of being accused of acting on illegal inform-

ation. The best procedure is: against opponents who play a comprehensible system, either ask no questions at all or say at the end, 'Did any of your bids have a special meaning?' When opponents play a complicated system, ask at every turn.

3. A technical point: refrain from pointless doubles as the bidding proceeds. For example, if the opponent on your right bids the fourth suit, or responds to a Blackwood 4NT, don't imagine that it is clever to insert a double because you hold something like Q 10 9 x x of the suit called. Even international players make this childish mistake. If you double a conventional bid the next player has three options instead of one: he may pass, he may redouble, he may bid. (Specific lead-directing doubles are another matter.)

4. Tactical bidding, such as pretending to a control you do not possess, is one thing; psychic bidding is another. On the whole, avoid it. If you bid spades when you hold neither length nor strength, one of two things can happen: you will run into a big penalty or the bid will succeed and there will be grumbles, not to say accusations. In particular, avoid 'experimenting' when you are not doing well in a pairs event. You are on a loser either way: the bid may succeed and your opponents will be annoyed, or it may be a disaster and then there will be complaints from pairs who will say that you 'chucked' points to their rivals.

5. In pairs, especially, make what you judge to be the normal lead against any ordinary contract. You start from the assumption (I hope) that you and your partner defend better than most of the pairs who come your way; don't risk throwing away that advantage by making a lead that may turn out to be disastrous.

6. Similarly, when partner has made the opening lead, follow his line of defence unless you are quite sure than another line would be better. There are two reasons for this: you don't want to risk annoying your partner; and when the direction the play will take is uncertain you don't want to embark on a line of play that will not occur to other players.

7. As every player is told when he learns the game, the time to think is at trick one. *Always* do this, however simple the hand may seem and however obvious your play at this point may be. An opponent cannot complain if at trick one you think about playing a singleton, for example. Suppose, also, that partner leads an intermediate card, dummy goes down with x x x, and you hold A x or A 10 x x. With A x you will always play the ace, of course, with A 10 x x you may need to consider. For various reasons, don't play quickly with one holding, thoughtfully with the other.

8. You will often have difficult discards when an opponent plays off a long suit. Do your thinking early. It is perfectly proper to consider how you will discard on the later rounds. Also, when you hold the majority of the defensive strength, and this has not been revealed by the bidding, think early on about the problems that may follow – whether it may be necessary to bare a king or ace, for example. Don't wait until the problem confronts you and then go into a trance.

9. Constant signalling, whether to show length or strength, is the mark of second-rate players. Trust your partner to know what is going on; don't add to the declarer's information. And remember, when you can afford it, to play the card you are already known to hold.

10. Whatever happens in the play, the best comment is no comment. In one of his books Terence Reese describes an occasion when an Italian pair in the European Championship bid a grand slam in notrumps with a suit wide open and lost about 900. Not a word was spoken, and their French opponents were so nonplussed that they scarcely played a right card for the rest of the session.

A final word: despite the long discussions in some magazines about points of law and procedure, and despite the example of some sports, remember that bridge is a game.

Acknowledgements

It is perilously easy, when noting that a certain line of defence would have worked well, to overlook the case for a different line of play. I am particularly grateful to Gus Calderwood for examining all the deals in that light.

As on previous occasions, I must thank the editors of Faber and Faber for checking my imperfect English.

M.H.

Part I

Deals 1–31

1   **Good Start**

Dealer South   Love all

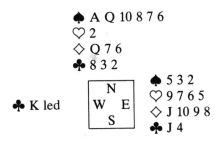

♠ A Q 10 8 7 6
♡ 2
◇ Q 7 6
♣ 8 3 2

♠ 5 3 2
♡ 9 7 6 5
◇ J 10 9 8
♣ J 4

♣ K led

South	West	North	East
1♡	dble	1♠	No
3♡	No	3♠	No
4♡	No	No	No

West begins with ♣ A K and a low club, which you ruff. South has followed with the 9, 10 and queen. What do you lead now?

This is not an entirely new type of problem, but I am sure you would like to be away to a good start. You are a little suspicious of the jack of diamonds? Yes, well, to earn full marks you must know what you are doing – and why.

Answer 1

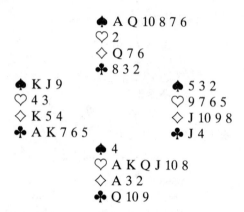

♠ A Q 10 8 7 6
♡ 2
♢ Q 7 6
♣ 8 3 2

♠ K J 9
♡ 4 3
♢ K 5 4
♣ A K 7 6 5

♠ 5 3 2
♡ 9 7 6 5
♢ J 10 9 8
♣ J 4

♠ 4
♡ A K Q J 10 8
♢ A 3 2
♣ Q 10 9

South plays in four hearts after West has doubled the opening one heart. (South ought to have been in 3NT as the bidding went, but at rubber bridge the honours were tempting.)

The defence begins with ace, king and another club, East ruffing. It is just possible that at the table you would have returned the jack of diamonds, but no doubt you can see why that would be wrong. South would go up with the ace and run the hearts, causing West much discomfiture.

The only sensible play at trick four is a spade, destroying the entry for a squeeze.

2   A Matter of Tempo

Dealer South   Game all

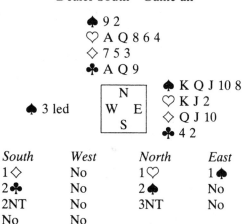

♠ 9 2
♡ A Q 8 6 4
♢ 7 5 3
♣ A Q 9

♠ 3 led

N
W   E
S

♠ K Q J 10 8
♡ K J 2
♢ Q J 10
♣ 4 2

South	West	North	East
1♢	No	1♡	1♠
2♣	No	2♠	No
2NT	No	3NT	No
No	No		

West leads a low spade and South decides to win so that he will later have a card of exit. Four top clubs are played and a heart is thrown from dummy. The question is, How should East discard on the third and fourth rounds?

Answer 2

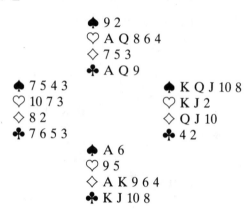

```
                    ♠ 9 2
                    ♡ A Q 8 6 4
                    ◇ 7 5 3
                    ♣ A Q 9
   ♠ 7 5 4 3                        ♠ K Q J 10 8
   ♡ 10 7 3                         ♡ K J 2
   ◇ 8 2                            ◇ Q J 10
   ♣ 7 6 5 3                        ♣ 4 2
                    ♠ A 6
                    ♡ 9 5
                    ◇ A K 9 6 4
                    ♣ K J 10 8
```

South plays in 3NT after East, who is vulnerable, has over-called in spades. West leads ♠ 3 and South wins the first trick so that he will have an exit card. Four clubs are played off and East has to find two discards.

East is in a situation here that a regular player will meet a hundred times in a year. He knows (a) that declarer has eight tricks on top, and (b) that he will have no safe discard on the last club.

It is very important to recognize this early on and be prepared to discard smoothly. You *know*, if you think about it, that you will be obliged to discard two hearts. Your best chance is to persuade declarer that you are 5–4–2–2. Your first two discards are ♡ 2 and ♡ J, or the other way round. South will cash ace and king of diamonds, and now ◇ 10 and ◇ Q are probably the best cards to choose. There is then a fair chance that South will exit in spades, hoping that the suit is blocked and that you will be forced to lead into ♡ A Q.

Anyone could find this defence if he thought about it. The whole art lies in thinking ahead and playing at normal tempo.

3   A Trifle Odd

Dealer South   E–W vulnerable

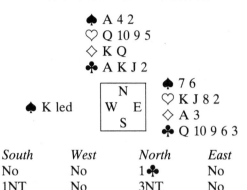

♠ A 4 2
♡ Q 10 9 5
◇ K Q
♣ A K J 2

♠ 7 6
♡ K J 8 2
◇ A 3
♣ Q 10 9 6 3

♠ K led

South	West	North	East
No	No	1♣	No
1NT	No	3NT	No
No	No		

West led the king of spades, which in the system was a 'strong' card, indicating K Q 10 x x or a suit headed by K Q J. Dummy played low and East dropped the 7, which denied the jack and was the right card from a doubleton. South followed suit with the 8 of spades. West then switched to the 9 of diamonds. East won and returned a spade, which was won in dummy.

Declarer cashed the queen of diamonds and followed with the 10 of hearts. East contributed the jack and the rest of the story, from the angle of the defence, was improper, South ending with overtricks.

Where did the defence go wrong?

Answer 3

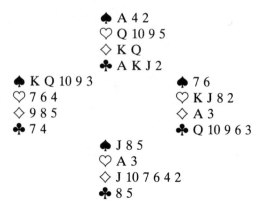

```
              ♠ A 4 2
              ♡ Q 10 9 5
              ◇ K Q
              ♣ A K J 2
♠ K Q 10 9 3              ♠ 7 6
♡ 7 6 4                   ♡ K J 8 2
◇ 9 8 5                   ◇ A 3
♣ 7 4                     ♣ Q 10 9 6 3
              ♠ J 8 5
              ♡ A 3
              ◇ J 10 7 6 4 2
              ♣ 8 5
```

North opened one club in third position and you may think that South's response of 1NT was a trifle odd. However, he was playing in a pairs and it was quite a good idea to bid 1NT, making it difficult for West to enter the bidding.

West led the king of spades, which held the first trick, and switched to the 9 of diamonds. East hastily led his second spade and followed this, two tricks later, by covering the 10 of hearts with the jack. This was poor play, but the real mistake was the return of the second spade instead of the king of hearts, which would have removed South's entry while the diamonds were blocked.

The return of the king of hearts at trick three is a type of play generally called a Deschapelles coup. Strictly speaking, it is a Merrimac coup. The Deschapelles is the play of a high card that establishes an entry card for the player's partner. It occurs in this type of position:

```
              A x
Q x x x                   K x x x
              J 10 x
```

Here the lead of the king by East ensures an early entry for his partner.

18

4   **Choice of Twelve**

Dealer South   Love all

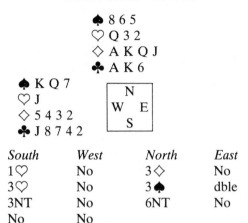

♠ 8 6 5
♡ Q 3 2
◇ A K Q J
♣ A K 6

♠ K Q 7
♡ J
◇ 5 4 3 2
♣ J 8 7 4 2

South	West	North	East
1♡	No	3◇	No
3♡	No	3♠	dble
3NT	No	6NT	No
No	No		

North's three spades was the sort of bid that some players make in the hope of averting a dangerous lead. The attempt misfired when East doubled and West led the king of spades against the eventual slam. East played the jack and declarer the 2.

What should West lead at trick two?

Answer 4

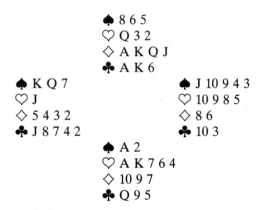

♠ 8 6 5
♡ Q 3 2
◇ A K Q J
♣ A K 6

♠ K Q 7
♡ J
◇ 5 4 3 2
♣ J 8 7 4 2

♠ J 10 9 4 3
♡ 10 9 8 5
◇ 8 6
♣ 10 3

♠ A 2
♡ A K 7 6 4
◇ 10 9 7
♣ Q 9 5

South played in 6NT after North had bid spades in an unsuccessful attempt to avert a spade lead.

On the king of spades East played the jack and West continued gaily with the queen. This proved a calamity, because South won, played four diamonds and three clubs, then ace and queen of hearts. East, meanwhile, had been forced either to unguard the hearts or part with the 10 of spades.

West made a typical error when he followed the king of spades with the queen. To prevent any possibility of a squeeze against his partner, he must lead the 7 of spades at trick two; or, indeed, any card in his hand except for the queen of spades!

5   Confirming the Message

Dealer North   Love all

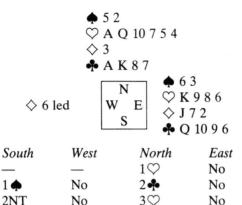

♠ 5 2
♡ A Q 10 7 5 4
◇ 3
♣ A K 8 7

◇ 6 led

♠ 6 3
♡ K 9 8 6
◇ J 7 2
♣ Q 10 9 6

South	West	North	East
—	—	1♡	No
1♠	No	2♣	No
2NT	No	3♡	No
3NT	No	No	No

Partner's lead of the 6 of diamonds runs to the jack and queen. South runs the jack of hearts and follows with a second heart, on which partner discards the 5 of diamonds. You win this trick with the king of hearts. What do you do next?

Answer 5

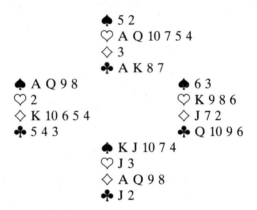

♠ 5 2
♡ A Q 10 7 5 4
◇ 3
♣ A K 8 7

♠ A Q 9 8
♡ 2
◇ K 10 6 5 4
♣ 5 4 3

♠ 6 3
♡ K 9 8 6
◇ J 7 2
♣ Q 10 9 6

♠ K J 10 7 4
♡ J 3
◇ A Q 9 8
♣ J 2

South plays in 3NT after his partner has bid hearts and clubs. A club lead would have been best, but West has chosen his third best diamond, with the idea that this may encourage his partner to lead a spade at the first opportunity. He is able to confirm this message by discarding a diamond on the second round of hearts.

Taking the hint, you return a spade when in with the king of hearts. West wins and leads a club. You win with the queen and return a second spade. West exits with a club and the declarer is unhappily placed. If he wins in dummy he will lose a fifth trick at the finish, and he will fare no better if he lets the club run to the jack.

6   Don't Even Think

Dealer South   Game all

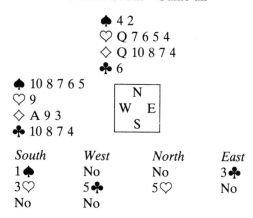

♠ 4 2
♡ Q 7 6 5 4
♢ Q 10 8 7 4
♣ 6

♠ 10 8 7 6 5
♡ 9
♢ A 9 3
♣ 10 8 7 4

South	West	North	East
1♠	No	No	3♣
3♡	5♣	5♡	No
No	No		

West leads a club to partner's king (which may be a false card), and East returns the 9 of spades, taken by the ace. South draws the trumps in three rounds, then plays three more top spades and ruffs a spade. Now you can see:

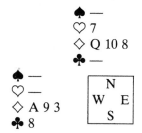

♠ —
♡ 7
♢ Q 10 8
♣ —

♠ —
♡ —
♢ A 9 3
♣ 8

South plays a diamond to the king. Were you ready for this? How do you play?

Answer 6

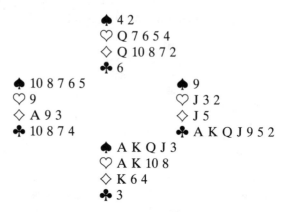

```
                    ♠ 4 2
                    ♡ Q 7 6 5 4
                    ◇ Q 10 8 7 2
                    ♣ 6
  ♠ 10 8 7 6 5                      ♠ 9
  ♡ 9                               ♡ J 3 2
  ◇ A 9 3                           ◇ J 5
  ♣ 10 8 7 4                        ♣ A K Q J 9 5 2
                    ♠ A K Q J 3
                    ♡ A K 10 8
                    ◇ K 6 4
                    ♣ 3
```

South plays in five hearts after East has shown long clubs and West has supported him. West leads a club and East wins with the king. (This, in general, is sound play, because to win with the jack would assist the declarer to read the lie of the cards.) East exits with a spade.

After drawing trumps, cashing three more spades, and ruffing the fifth round, South leads a diamond to the king. In this type of situation it is often good play to duck, encouraging the declarer to finesse the 10 on the next round. That would be foolish here because, if you are awake, you know that East has one diamond and three clubs left; if you duck, or if you even think about it, you are lost.

When you win with the ace, do you return the 9 or the 3? It is just a psychological question, of course. Most defenders would return the 9, hoping to create the impression that they held A J 9. Against an experienced declarer I would be more inclined to lead the 3, trying to look like a man who held A J 3.

7   **Double Dummy Line**

Dealer South   Game all

♠ 4
♡ 9 8 5
♢ 10 9 3 2
♣ A 7 6 5 4

```
    N
W     E
    S
```

South	West	North	East
1♠	No	2♢	2♡
3♢	No	3♡	No
3♠	No	5♠	No
6♠	No	No	No

It is the sort of contract that may well depend on the lead. What is your selection, and why?

Answer 7

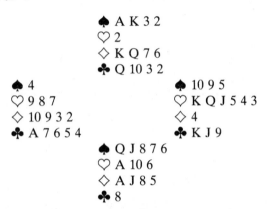

♠ A K 3 2
♡ 2
♢ K Q 7 6
♣ Q 10 3 2

♠ 4
♡ 9 8 7
♢ 10 9 3 2
♣ A 7 6 5 4

♠ 10 9 5
♡ K Q J 5 4 3
♢ 4
♣ K J 9

♠ Q J 8 7 6
♡ A 10 6
♢ A J 8 5
♣ 8

North–South reach six spades after an auction in which diamonds have been bid and supported. You have to find a good lead.

They must be prepared for a heart lead and, as no one has mentioned clubs, it is fairly certain that they are not afraid of that suit either. There is no reason to suppose that a trump will cause them any embarrassment.

What about a diamond? The suit has been bid and supported, and while you don't expect partner to be void he may well hold a singleton. In this case a diamond lead may prevent the coming and going needed for any sort of ruffing game.

The diamond lead is, in fact, ruinous. Yes, declarer can succeed at double dummy by playing East for 10 9 x of trumps, but there is no reason why he should do anything so unlikely.

8   **Early Entry**

Dealer South   N–S vulnerable

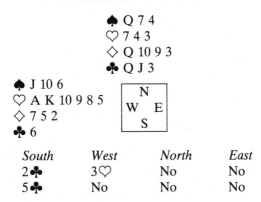

♠ Q 7 4
♡ 7 4 3
♢ Q 10 9 3
♣ Q J 3

♠ J 10 6
♡ A K 10 9 8 5
♢ 7 5 2
♣ 6

South	West	North	East
2♣	3♡	No	No
5♣	No	No	No

West leads the king of hearts; 2 from partner, queen from declarer. What should West play now?

The deal occurred in a match between England and Northern Ireland. At my table North, not unreasonably, went to six clubs. The opponents mistakenly sacrificed and lost 300.

Answer 8

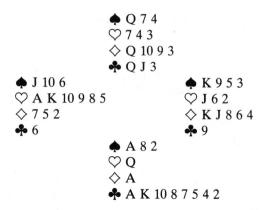

```
              ♠ Q 7 4
              ♡ 7 4 3
              ◇ Q 10 9 3
              ♣ Q J 3
♠ J 10 6                        ♠ K 9 5 3
♡ A K 10 9 8 5                  ♡ J 6 2
◇ 7 5 2                         ◇ K J 8 6 4
♣ 6                             ♣ 9
              ♠ A 8 2
              ♡ Q
              ◇ A
              ♣ A K 10 8 7 5 4 2
```

Defending against five clubs, West led the king of hearts and continued with the ace. South ruffed high, cashed the ace of diamonds, and used the three trump entries to dummy to establish a diamond winner for a spade discard.

West's heart continuation was certainly weak. He might have played a spade, but in some cases this would establish a spade winner for the declarer, who might have held such as A 9 8. Perhaps it wasn't easy to see that a trump at trick two would deprive the declarer of a necessary entry to dummy? South can cash the ace of diamonds and cross twice to the dummy, but twice is not enough.

9 **Breaking Up**

Dealer South   Game all

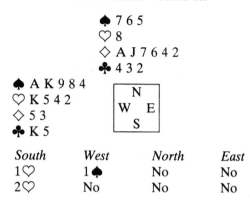

South	West	North	East
South	*West*	*North*	*East*
1♡	1♠	No	No
2♡	No	No	No

You begin with ace, king and another spade. Partner, who held ♠ J 3, ruffs the third round and leads the queen of clubs. South plays the 9 and you the 5. East follows with the jack of clubs. South wins, knocks out your king of hearts, and makes the contract.

You are not aware that you have done anything wrong, but your partner is looking thoughtful. Why?

Answer 9

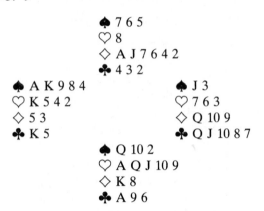

♠ 7 6 5
♡ 8
♢ A J 7 6 4 2
♣ 4 3 2

♠ A K 9 8 4
♡ K 5 4 2
♢ 5 3
♣ K 5

♠ J 3
♡ 7 6 3
♢ Q 10 9
♣ Q J 10 8 7

♠ Q 10 2
♡ A Q J 10 9
♢ K 8
♣ A 9 6

South played in two hearts after West had overcalled in spades. The defence began with three rounds of spades, East ruffing the third round. The queen of clubs held the next trick. South won the club continuation and forced out the king of hearts. He ruffed the next spade and drew trumps. East, meanwhile, was squeezed in the minor suits. At the finish South held two diamonds and a club, North ♢ A J 7, and East had to find a discard from ♢ Q 10 9 and ♣ 10.

West was surprised when his partner blamed him for the defence. West should, in fact, overtake the queen of clubs with the king and lead a diamond. When he comes in with the king of hearts he leads another diamond, breaking up the entries for a squeeze. Not too difficult, if you think about it.

Note, too, that a diamond from *East* at trick 4 is also an effective play.

10   Easier in the Long Suit

Dealer South   Game all

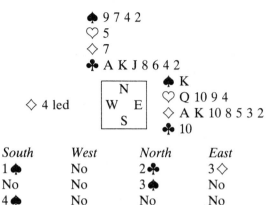

```
              ♠ 9 7 4 2
              ♡ 5
              ♢ 7
              ♣ A K J 8 6 4 2
                              ♠ K
              ┌─────────┐     ♡ Q 10 9 4
  ♢ 4 led     │    N    │     ♢ A K 10 8 5 3 2
              │ W     E │     ♣ 10
              │    S    │
              └─────────┘
```

South	*West*	*North*	*East*
1♠	No	2♣	3♢
No	No	3♠	No
4♠	No	No	No

An unbalanced hand such as North's seldom plays well in anything but the long suit. On this occasion five clubs would have been an easier contract than four spades.

West led the 4 of diamonds, East played the king and declarer the jack. Sitting East, what would be your line of defence?

Answer 10

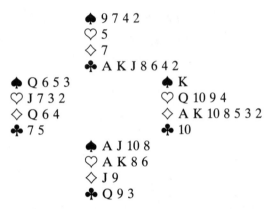

♠ 9 7 4 2
♡ 5
♢ 7
♣ A K J 8 6 4 2

♠ Q 6 5 3
♡ J 7 3 2
♢ Q 6 4
♣ 7 5

♠ K
♡ Q 10 9 4
♢ A K 10 8 5 3 2
♣ 10

♠ A J 10 8
♡ A K 8 6
♢ J 9
♣ Q 9 3

South plays in four spades after East has overcalled in diamonds. West leads a low diamond to the king, on which South drops the jack.

Many players would switch to a heart, but South is sure to hold the ace and the only real chance is to attempt to weaken the dummy. East should play another high diamond. This will give the defence good chances if West holds something like Q x x x in the trump suit.

South will probably take the force in dummy and lead a spade to the king and ace. If he leads a second spade now he can be defeated. West will hold off and the declarer will now be flat on his back (assuming that West has unblocked in diamonds). West will win the next spade and lead a diamond, which South has to ruff. Now West has the long trump and will ruff the third round of clubs.

The best play for declarer, after ruffing a diamond in dummy and playing a spade to the king and ace, is to abandon trumps and play on clubs.

11 **End of Dream**

Dealer North   Love all

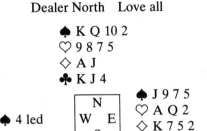

♠ K Q 10 2
♡ 9 8 7 5
♢ A J
♣ K J 4

♠ 4 led

♠ J 9 7 5
♡ A Q 2
♢ K 7 5 2
♣ 8 7

South	West	North	East
—	—	1♡	No
1♠	No	4♠	No
No	No		

The North hand is a little awkward if you are playing a strong notrump. Either one spade or one club strikes me as preferable to one heart. The raise to four spades was, of course, ridiculous.

West led the 4 of spades and my 9 – I was East – was headed by South's ace. The declarer led a low heart at trick two. My partner went in with the 10 and I let him hold the trick, expecting a switch to diamonds. Instead, he led a second trump, won in dummy. So South had responded in a three-card suit.

The declarer's next move was another heart from dummy. I won this and could see:

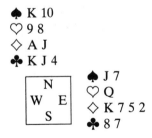

♠ K 10
♡ 9 8
♢ A J
♣ K J 4

♠ J 7
♡ Q
♢ K 7 5 2
♣ 8 7

What was the right play now?

Answer 11

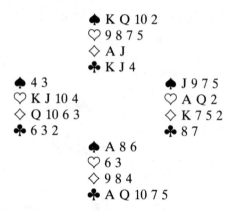

♠ K Q 10 2
♡ 9 8 7 5
◇ A J
♣ K J 4

♠ 4 3
♡ K J 10 4
◇ Q 10 6 3
♣ 6 3 2

♠ J 9 7 5
♡ A Q 2
◇ K 7 5 2
♣ 8 7

♠ A 8 6
♡ 6 3
◇ 9 8 4
♣ A Q 10 7 5

When North opened one heart, South chose to respond one spade. I imagine he hoped to play in 3NT and avert what might be a dangerous attack. However, North ended this dream by raising to four spades. Personally, I don't mind a raise to three with these good trumps, though many players would bid only two.

West led a trump and my 9 lost to the ace. South led a heart, my partner won and played a second trump to dummy's king. Still aiming for a heart ruff, South led another heart, which I won with the ace.

From the way the play was going, I could see that South held good clubs and I played a diamond now. This was very necessary, because if I played a neutral heart or club he could take a heart ruff, force out my jack of spades, and make the rest.

12   **Free Choice**

Dealer South   Game all

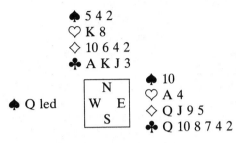

♠ 5 4 2
♡ K 8
◇ 10 6 4 2
♣ A K J 3

♠ 10
♡ A 4
◇ Q J 9 5
♣ Q 10 8 7 4 2

♠ Q led

South	West	North	East
2♡	No	3♡	No
3♠	No	4♣	No
4NT	No	5◇	No
6♡	No	No	No

South's two hearts is an Acol two-bid, showing a powerful hand. North's three hearts sets the suit. Three spades and four clubs are cue bids.

West leads the queen of spades (presumably from Q J) and South wins with the ace. He leads the 9 of hearts, 5 from West, king from dummy. What will you do now?

Answer 12

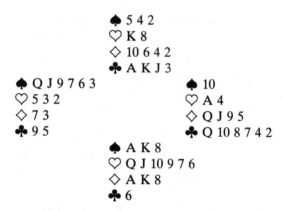

♠ 5 4 2
♥ K 8
♦ 10 6 4 2
♣ A K J 3

♠ Q J 9 7 6 3 ♠ 10
♥ 5 3 2 ♥ A 4
♦ 7 3 ♦ Q J 9 5
♣ 9 5 ♣ Q 10 8 7 4 2

♠ A K 8
♥ Q J 10 9 7 6
♦ A K 8
♣ 6

South, who has opened with an Acol two hearts, plays in six hearts, and West leads the queen of spades. Declarer wins and leads the 9 of hearts; 5 from West, king from dummy.

East cannot be sure whether his partner's 5 of hearts is from a doubleton or is the beginning of an echo to show three. In any case, it cannot be wrong to win. The danger of a diamond now is that if declarer holds A K of both spades and diamonds, together with a singleton club, he may develop a squeeze against East in the minor suits. Suppose, for example, that South has three diamonds and a singleton club. He will run the trumps and the king of spades, and East will be dead.

It can hardly cost to return a club, because South has two tricks in the suit already. (Since he bid a Blackwood 4NT, he is most unlikely to be void in clubs.) Any club will do. South will make the jack and king, but West will surely be able to ruff the third round.

Alternative Plan

Dealer South   N–S vulnerable

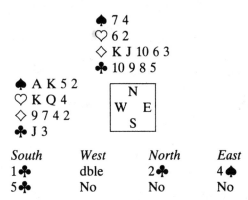

♠ 7 4
♡ 6 2
◇ K J 10 6 3
♣ 10 9 8 5

♠ A K 5 2
♡ K Q 4
◇ 9 7 4 2
♣ J 3

South	West	North	East
1♣	dble	2♣	4♠
5♣	No	No	No

West led the king of spades and continued with a low spade when his partner played the queen. South ruffed and played a diamond to the 10, which held. He led the 10 of clubs from dummy, 4 from East, queen from hand.

Sitting West, have you any special plan to defeat this contract?

Answer 13

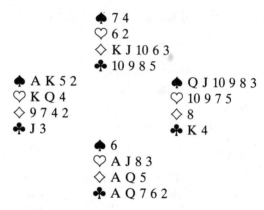

```
                    ♠ 7 4
                    ♡ 6 2
                    ◇ K J 10 6 3
                    ♣ 10 9 8 5
♠ A K 5 2                        ♠ Q J 10 9 8 3
♡ K Q 4                         ♡ 10 9 7 5
◇ 9 7 4 2                       ◇ 8
♣ J 3                           ♣ K 4
                    ♠ 6
                    ♡ A J 8 3
                    ◇ A Q 5
                    ♣ A Q 7 6 2
```

South plays in five clubs after West has doubled the opening bid and East has bid four spades.

The defence begins with two rounds of spades. South ruffs, crosses to the 10 of diamonds and leads the 10 of clubs to the queen.

The question asked was, 'Sitting West, have you any special plan to defeat this contract?' Admittedly, this rather gives away the point. West should try the effect of dropping the jack of clubs under the queen. Imagining that this is a singleton, South may try to enter dummy with another diamond. East will ruff and the defence will still come to a trick in hearts.

If the clubs were indeed 3–1, South's play would be right. He would pick up the trumps, cash the ace of diamonds, and concede a heart, so losing just one heart and one spade.

14   **Hardly the Form**

Dealer South   E–W vulnerable

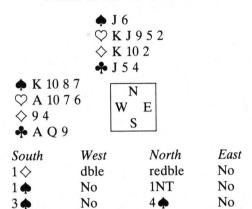

♠ J 6
♡ K J 9 5 2
◇ K 10 2
♣ J 5 4

♠ K 10 8 7
♡ A 10 7 6
◇ 9 4
♣ A Q 9

South	West	North	East
1◇	dble	redble	No
1♠	No	1NT	No
3♠	No	4♠	No
No	No		

West, who had a rather awkward choice of lead, began with the ace of hearts. South ruffed, led a diamond to the king, and took a club discard on the king of hearts. He came back to the ace of diamonds and led a low spade. How should West play now?

Answer 14

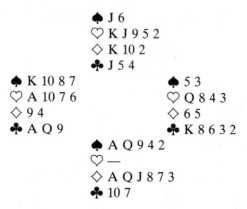

♠ J 6
♡ K J 9 5 2
◇ K 10 2
♣ J 5 4

♠ K 10 8 7   ♠ 5 3
♡ A 10 7 6   ♡ Q 8 4 3
◇ 9 4   ◇ 6 5
♣ A Q 9   ♣ K 8 6 3 2

♠ A Q 9 4 2
♡ —
◇ A Q J 8 7 3
♣ 10 7

South played in four spades and West made the unfortunate lead of the ace of hearts. South ruffed, crossed to the king of diamonds, and took a discard on the king of hearts. He came back to hand with a diamond and led a low spade.

Since South has already ruffed once, it is fairly clear, I would have thought, that West should go up with the king of spades and switch to clubs. After ruffing the second round (he has discarded one club) South is down to two trumps and has no play for the contract.

Not a difficult defence, to be sure, but in what they call a preliminary international trial I saw West play low on the spade lead. South, naturally, made the jack and ace, then played on diamonds, losing just one club and two trumps.

North suggested that his partner might have tried a low spade from hand at trick two. This doesn't help. Knowing that South is going to take a discard on the king of hearts, West must go in with the king of spades and attack the clubs.

Hobson's Choice

Dealer South   Love all

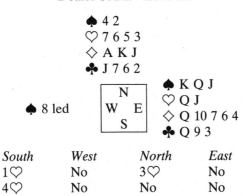

♠ 4 2
♡ 7 6 5 3
♢ A K J
♣ J 7 6 2

♠ 8 led

♠ K Q J
♡ Q J
♢ Q 10 7 6 4
♣ Q 9 3

South	West	North	East
1♡	No	3♡	No
4♡	No	No	No

West leads the 8 of spades (second best from a bad suit) and your jack is allowed to hold. You switch to the queen of trumps. South wins, plays ace of spades and ruffs the 10, then leads a heart from dummy. You play the jack, which to your surprise is allowed to hold, West completing an echo. Now you can see:

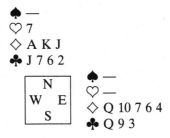

♠ —
♡ 7
♢ A K J
♣ J 7 6 2

♠ —
♡ —
♢ Q 10 7 6 4
♣ Q 9 3

What do you play now?

Answer 15

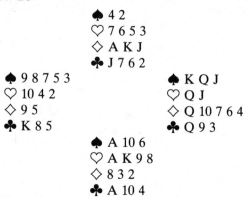

♠ 4 2
♡ 7 6 5 3
◇ A K J
♣ J 7 6 2

♠ 9 8 7 5 3
♡ 10 4 2
◇ 9 5
♣ K 8 5

♠ K Q J
♡ Q J
◇ Q 10 7 6 4
♣ Q 9 3

♠ A 10 6
♡ A K 9 8
◇ 8 3 2
♣ A 10 4

South played in four hearts and West led a spade, won by the jack. South won the trump return, made the ace of spades, took a spade ruff, and allowed East to hold the next trick with the jack of hearts. The position was then:

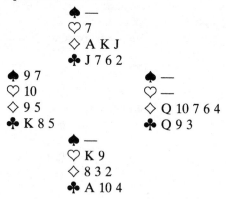

♠ —
♡ 7
◇ A K J
♣ J 7 6 2

♠ 9 7
♡ 10
◇ 9 5
♣ K 8 5

♠ —
♡ —
◇ Q 10 7 6 4
♣ Q 9 3

♠ —
♡ K 9
◇ 8 3 2
♣ A 10 4

Taking the view that a diamond was sure to lose a trick, while a club might not, East returned a club. West won and led a diamond. South won in dummy, finessed the 10 of clubs, and discarded his losing diamond on the thirteenth club.

'Why didn't you lead a diamond when you were in?' West demanded. 'At least that couldn't give away *two* tricks.'

16 Hound Dog

Dealer East   N–S vulnerable

<pre>
            ♠ Q 5
            ♡ 10 7 5 4
            ◇ A Q J 9 7 6 5
            ♣ —
♠ A 10 4 3
♡ 2   N
◇ K 10 8   W   E
♣ J 9 7 6 5   S
</pre>

South	West	North	East
—	—	—	2♡
2♠	No	3◇	No
3♡	No	3♠	No
4♠	No	No	No

Your partner's two-heart opening was in the 7 to 10 range.
You lead your singleton heart, which runs to the 9 and ace. South
plays a spade to the queen and returns a spade to the jack and
ace, partner following suit. Judging now that it is more important
to disrupt communications than to attack clubs, you lead the 10
of diamonds. Dummy's queen wins, partner playing the 4 and
declarer the 3.

A heart is led from dummy. Partner wins and you discard the
8 of diamonds. Now you can see:

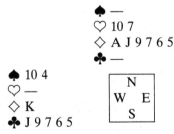

<pre>
            ♠ —
            ♡ 10 7
            ◇ A J 9 7 6 5
            ♣ —
♠ 10 4
♡ —   N
◇ K   W   E
♣ J 9 7 6 5   S
</pre>

East leads a heart and South ruffs with the king. What do you
do now?

Answer 16

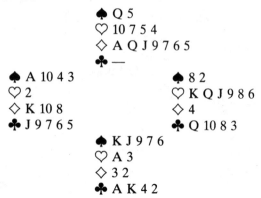

♠ Q 5
♡ 10 7 5 4
♢ A Q J 9 7 6 5
♣ —

♠ A 10 4 3   ♠ 8 2
♡ 2   ♡ K Q J 9 8 6
♢ K 10 8   ♢ 4
♣ J 9 7 6 5   ♣ Q 10 8 3

♠ K J 9 7 6
♡ A 3
♢ 3 2
♣ A K 4 2

South plays in four spades after East has opened with a weak two hearts. Declarer wins the heart lead, plays a spade to the queen and returns a spade to the jack and ace. You lead a diamond, won in dummy, and South exits with a heart, on which you discard ♢ 8. The situation now is:

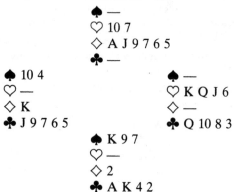

♠ —
♡ 10 7
♢ A J 9 7 6 5
♣ —

♠ 10 4   ♠ —
♡ —   ♡ K Q J 6
♢ K   ♢ —
♣ J 9 7 6 5   ♣ Q 10 8 3

♠ K 9 7
♡ —
♢ 2
♣ A K 4 2

East exits with a heart and South ruffs with the king of spades. At the table West, like a hound dog on the trail, discards his last diamond. A mistake! South simply leads a trump and makes the rest. You must discard a club and then, when in with the 10 of spades, you can exit with a diamond and make two more tricks.

In Touch

Dealer South   N–S vulnerable

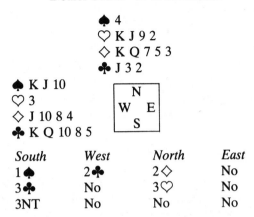

♠ 4
♡ K J 9 2
♢ K Q 7 5 3
♣ J 3 2

♠ K J 10
♡ 3
♢ J 10 8 4
♣ K Q 10 8 5

South	West	North	East
1♠	2♣	2♢	No
3♣	No	3♡	No
3NT	No	No	No

Fearing the worst, you lead the king of clubs and dummy turns up with the dreaded J x x. Partner plays the 4 and South wins with the ace. You are playing in a pairs, by the way.

The declarer plays off four rounds of diamonds, East discarding the 8 of hearts, followed by two low spades, and South a low spade on the fourth round.

In with the fourth diamond, you can see:

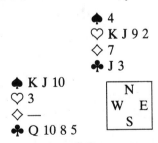

♠ 4
♡ K J 9 2
♢ 7
♣ J 3

♠ K J 10
♡ 3
♢ —
♣ Q 10 8 5

What do you play now?

Answer 17

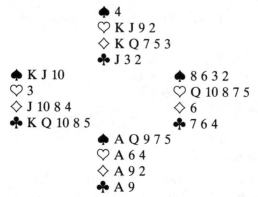

♠ 4
♡ K J 9 2
♢ K Q 7 5 3
♣ J 3 2

♠ K J 10   ♠ 8 6 3 2
♡ 3   ♡ Q 10 8 7 5
♢ J 10 8 4   ♢ 6
♣ K Q 10 8 5   ♣ 7 6 4

♠ A Q 9 7 5
♡ A 6 4
♢ A 9 2
♣ A 9

South played in 3NT after West had overcalled in clubs. The king of clubs was taken by the ace and declarer played four rounds of diamonds. This left:

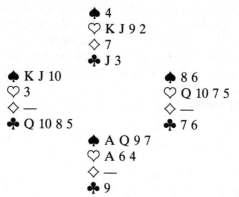

♠ 4
♡ K J 9 2
♢ 7
♣ J 3

♠ K J 10   ♠ 8 6
♡ 3   ♡ Q 10 7 5
♢ —   ♢ —
♣ Q 10 8 5   ♣ 7 6

♠ A Q 9 7
♡ A 6 4
♢ —
♣ 9

Now West played ♣ Q and ♣ 5. On the fifth diamond East (I was East) had to throw a spade. Then came ♠ A, ♡ A and a heart to the 9 and 10. South had made a valuable overtrick.

'Is it better if I lead a heart when I'm in?' my partner asked.

'Probably not,' I answered. 'But I did play the 4 of clubs on the first trick. I would have petered with a doubleton. If you exit with the *10* of clubs we can hold them to nine tricks.'

18   Little Credit

Dealer East   E–W vulnerable

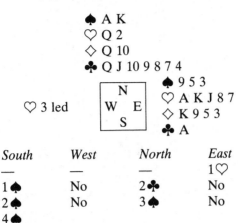

♠ A K
♡ Q 2
♢ Q 10
♣ Q J 10 9 8 7 4

♠ 9 5 3
♡ A K J 8 7
♢ K 9 5 3
♣ A

♡ 3 led

N
W   E
S

South	West	North	East
—	—	—	1♡
1♠	No	2♣	No
2♠	No	3♠	No
4♠			

North had a lot of points, but he couldn't be sure whether his queens would be worth much.

West led the 3 of hearts to East's king and South dropped the 10 on the second round. It looked as though the hearts were 5–4–2–2 and South was likely to hold the ace of diamonds and the king of clubs.

What should East do now?

Answer 18

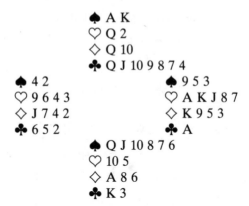

♠ A K
♥ Q 2
♦ Q 10
♣ Q J 10 9 8 7 4

♠ 4 2
♥ 9 6 4 3
♦ J 7 4 2
♣ 6 5 2

♠ 9 5 3
♥ A K J 8 7
♦ K 9 5 3
♣ A

♠ Q J 10 8 7 6
♥ 10 5
♦ A 8 6
♣ K 3

South played in four spades after East had opened one heart. West led the 3 of hearts and all followed to the ace and king.

As it happened, I held the East cards. It seemed as though South must hold the ace of diamonds and the king of clubs, so there was only one chance – that we could stick him in dummy and come to a club ruff. As I see these positions fairly quickly, I cashed the ace of clubs and followed with the king of diamonds. After making the top spades in dummy South had to let me ruff the second round of clubs. He was able to cross to ♢ Q later, but he was still one down.

I thought I might get a small compliment from my partner at rubber bridge, but no: 'I had only one point and it helped us to beat the contract,' he exclaimed. 'If South had held my jack of diamonds he would have unblocked the queen and had an entry to hand.

'You did marvellously,' I said.

19   Look for the Exit

Dealer North   Game all

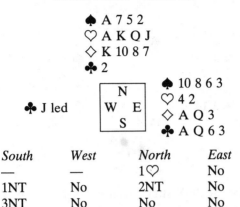

♠ A 7 5 2
♡ A K Q J
◇ K 10 8 7
♣ 2

♠ 10 8 6 3
♡ 4 2
◇ A Q 3
♣ A Q 6 3

♣ J led

South	West	North	East
—	—	1♡	No
1NT	No	2NT	No
3NT	No	No	No

West leads the jack of clubs, you encourage with the 6, and declarer plays low. West follows with the 10 of clubs and a diamond is discarded from dummy. What is your defensive plan?

49

Answer 19

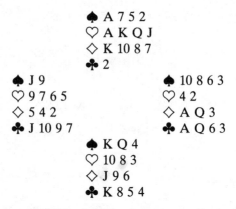

♠ A 7 5 2
♡ A K Q J
♢ K 10 8 7
♣ 2

♠ J 9
♡ 9 7 6 5
♢ 5 4 2
♣ J 10 9 7

♠ 10 8 6 3
♡ 4 2
♢ A Q 3
♣ A Q 6 3

♠ K Q 4
♡ 10 8 3
♢ J 9 6
♣ K 8 5 4

South plays in 3NT after North has opened one heart. West leads the jack of clubs, East plays the 6, and South plays low. West follows with the 10 of clubs, on which a diamond is thrown from dummy.

This is a fairly elementary – or at any rate a fairly common – situation. If East takes the ace and returns a third round, four rounds of hearts will be awkward for him. He will have to throw a diamond and a club, and then four rounds of spades will leave him on play.

It is no use blaming partner for not switching to a diamond at trick two. The aim on these hands where you may need to make awkward discards is to keep just one card of exit. On the second club you mustn't play the ace, you must play the queen. If South captures this you will be able to discard the ace of clubs on the fourth heart. And if South lets the queen of clubs hold, simply exit with a heart; you will have a defence against any line of play.

No Chance to Run

Dealer South   N–S vulnerable

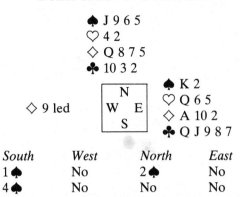

♠ J 9 6 5
♡ 4 2
◇ Q 8 7 5
♣ 10 3 2

◇ 9 led

N
W   E
S

♠ K 2
♡ Q 6 5
◇ A 10 2
♣ Q J 9 8 7

South	West	North	East
1♠	No	2♠	No
4♠	No	No	No

West leads the 9 of diamonds and a rather poor dummy goes down. Declarer covers with the queen of diamonds and you win with the ace. What is your next move?

Answer 20

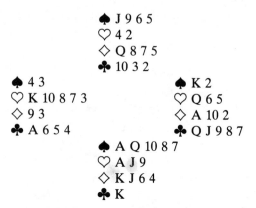

♠ J 9 6 5
♥ 4 2
♦ Q 8 7 5
♣ 10 3 2

♠ 4 3
♥ K 10 8 7 3
♦ 9 3
♣ A 6 5 4

♠ K 2
♥ Q 6 5
♦ A 10 2
♣ Q J 9 8 7

♠ A Q 10 8 7
♥ A J 9
♦ K J 6 4
♣ K

West leads the 9 of diamonds against four spades, the queen is played from dummy and you win with the ace.

It is easy to return the queen of clubs, but the danger of this is that West will continue the suit. Declarer will subsequently enter dummy with a heart ruff and take the spade finesse.

South has covered the 9 of diamonds because if you win and return a low diamond he intends to let it run to dummy. Then the spade finesse will win the contract.

You can frustrate this plan by returning the 10 of diamonds. Now South cannot reach the dummy without losing a trump trick – either to the king or to a diamond ruff.

21

No Guess

Dealer South   Love all

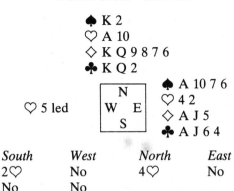

♠ K 2
♡ A 10
♢ K Q 9 8 7 6
♣ K Q 2

♡ 5 led

♠ A 10 7 6
♡ 4 2
♢ A J 5
♣ A J 6 4

South	West	North	East
2♡	No	4♡	No
No	No		

With three aces sitting over the strong hand, many players would have doubled in East's position. However, to give away the outstanding strength is often a mistake. In a pairs it might be right to double, but not at rubber bridge or in a team game.

South overtook dummy's 10 of hearts and led the 2 of diamonds, on which West played the 4. As West would not have played the 4 from 10 4 3, East let dummy's queen hold the trick. Declarer followed with the king of diamonds from dummy, doubtless hoping to drop the jack.

So you are in with the ace of diamonds. What is your next play?

Answer 21

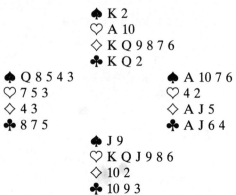

♠ K 2
♡ A 10
♢ K Q 9 8 7 6
♣ K Q 2

♠ Q 8 5 4 3
♡ 7 5 3
♢ 4 3
♣ 8 7 5

♠ A 10 7 6
♡ 4 2
♢ A J 5
♣ A J 6 4

♠ J 9
♡ K Q J 9 8 6
♢ 10 2
♣ 10 9 3

South opened with a weak two hearts and was raised to four hearts. When West led a trump, South overtook and led a diamond to the queen. This held and he followed with the king of diamonds, won by East's ace.

It was essential now to return the *jack* of clubs, to kill the later entry for the diamonds. South arrives at this position:

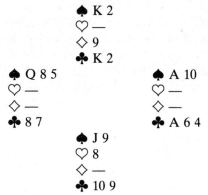

♠ K 2
♡ —
♢ 9
♣ K 2

♠ Q 8 5
♡ —
♢ —
♣ 8 7

♠ A 10
♡ —
♢ —
♣ A 6 4

♠ J 9
♡ 8
♢ —
♣ 10 9

If South leads the 10 of clubs, East holds off. The defenders make three more tricks, for one down.

22

On Your Own

Dealer South   E–W vulnerable

♠ A Q 9 8 7
♡ 10 2
◇ A 10 3
♣ A 5 4

```
    N
W       E
    S
```

South	West	North	East
1♡	dble	1♠	No
2NT	No	3NT	No
No	No		

Players talk about the 'luck of the lead'. This is an area where sometimes you will be unlucky, of course, but it is nevertheless an area where good players pick up a large number of points. It is clear on the present occasion that you will need to rely almost entirely on your own resources. What would you lead, and why?

Answer 22

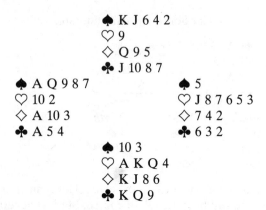

♠ K J 6 4 2
♡ 9
◇ Q 9 5
♣ J 10 8 7

♠ A Q 9 8 7   ♠ 5
♡ 10 2   ♡ J 8 7 6 5 3
◇ A 10 3   ◇ 7 4 2
♣ A 5 4   ♣ 6 3 2

♠ 10 3
♡ A K Q 4
◇ K J 8 6
♣ K Q 9

South plays in 3NT after West has doubled the opening one heart and North has bid spades.

There is no room for partner to hold much more than a jack and it would be a very long shot to find him with J x x x x x in one of the minors. Despite the spade bid on your left, there is a chance that you may establish three tricks in the suit. On the present hand either the ace of spades or the queen would hold the opposition to eight tricks. The ace is best because it covers the possibility of a singleton king in the South hand.

After the ace of spades you will continue with the queen, naturally, and you won't let them slip through a trick in one of the minors.

23

Not Classical

Dealer South   Love all

```
                    ♠ K 10 8 7 6
                    ♡ A Q 6 4
                    ◇ Q J
                    ♣ K 2
    ♠ 2
    ♡ 5 3 2              ┌─────────┐
    ◇ K 9 5 3 2         │   N     │
    ♣ J 10 9 8          │ W     E │
                        │   S     │
                        └─────────┘
```

South	West	North	East
1♠	No	4NT	No
5♡	No	6♠	No
No	No		

North's manoeuvres were not exactly classical. It is usually considered a mistake to bid 4NT when you hold an unprotected doubleton, and a response of five hearts won't tell you whether or not there are two immediate losers. However, opponents don't always find the killing lead, and that is what happened here.

South wins the club lead in dummy, draws one trump, and follows with the ace of clubs and a club ruff, spade to hand, club ruff, spade to hand. After two more rounds of trumps, on which two hearts are thrown from dummy, West and North hold:

```
                    ♠ —
                    ♡ A Q
                    ◇ Q J
                    ♣ —
    ♠ —
    ♡ 5 3
    ◇ K 9
    ♣ —
```

South leads his sixth (and last) trump. Sitting West, are you awake?

Answer 23

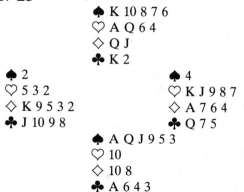

Playing in six spades, South won the club lead in dummy and arrived at this ending:

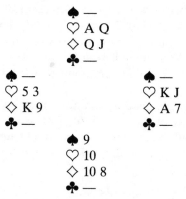

When South leads the last trump it is perilously easy for West to think 'well, the 3 of hearts won't make a trick' and discard a heart. Then a diamond is thrown from dummy and East has a severe problem. If he keeps ♢ A he will be thrown in, and if he discards it South may cash ♡ A and lead ♢ Q re-establishing a trick for ♢ 10.

It is, however, or should be, safe for West to discard the 9 of diamonds on the last trump. Then, if a diamond is thrown from dummy, East can hardly fail to discard the ace.

24   No Perturbation

Dealer East   N–S vulnerable

```
                  ♠ K 6
                  ♡ A J 10
                  ♢ 7 4 2
                  ♣ A K J 10 8
    ♠ A Q 9 5 4      ┌─────────┐
    ♡ 2              │    N    │
    ♢ 10 9 8         │  W   E  │
    ♣ 9 7 6 4        │    S    │
                     └─────────┘
```

South	West	North	East
—	—	—	3♡
3♠	No	5♣	No
No	dble	No	No
No			

I held the North cards during one of the Caransa tournaments that are held in Amsterdam. I thought of bidding 4NT over three spades, but I couldn't be sure that partner would take this as a general slam invitation. I think, on reflection, that I ought to have removed the double into 5NT, since West must have doubled on trump tricks.

West led his singleton heart and my partner, Paul Hackett, played the ace from dummy. He followed with a diamond to the ace and a low spade from hand. How should West play now?

Answer 24

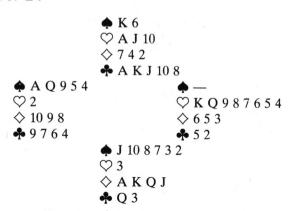

```
              ♠ K 6
              ♡ A J 10
              ◇ 7 4 2
              ♣ A K J 10 8
  ♠ A Q 9 5 4              ♠ —
  ♡ 2                      ♡ K Q 9 8 7 6 5 4
  ◇ 10 9 8                 ◇ 6 5 3
  ♣ 9 7 6 4                ♣ 5 2
              ♠ J 10 8 7 3 2
              ♡ 3
              ◇ A K Q J
              ♣ Q 3
```

South played in five spades doubled after East had opened three hearts. West led his singleton heart. The declarer won in dummy, played a diamond to the ace, and led a low spade.

It is not difficult to see that the safe defence is to win with the ace and return a spade. With Q 9 5 over declarer's J 10 8 you cannot fail to make two more tricks.

At the table West played low and was not unduly perturbed when declarer inserted dummy's 6. Two more diamonds were cashed and four clubs were played, South discarding a diamond and ruffing the fourth round. Only four cards were left and this was the trump position:

```
              ♠ K
  ♠ A Q 9 5              ♠ —
              ♠ J 10 8 3
```

West was held to two trump tricks and the contract was made.

25   **Protection Needed**

Dealer South   Love all

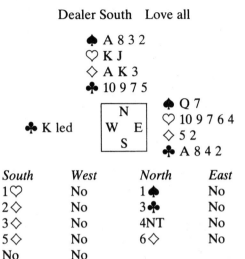

♠ A 8 3 2
♡ K J
♢ A K 3
♣ 10 9 7 5

♣ K led

♠ Q 7
♡ 10 9 7 6 4
♢ 5 2
♣ A 8 4 2

South	West	North	East
1♡	No	1♠	No
2♢	No	3♣	No
3♢	No	4NT	No
5♢	No	6♢	No
No	No		

This was not a particularly scientific auction, because from North's angle there might have been two losing clubs. North might have bought a little more time by simply bidding three hearts over South's three diamonds.

However, any anxiety on this point was relieved when West led the king of clubs and followed with the queen, which was ruffed by the declarer. South then drew three rounds of diamonds, East discarding a club on the third round.

Most players in the East position would have been surprised if someone had tapped them on the shoulder and said, 'You've done it in.' What was East's mistake?

Answer 25

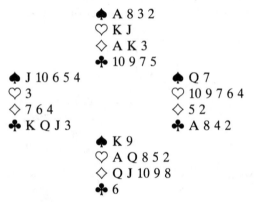

♠ A 8 3 2
♡ K J
♢ A K 3
♣ 10 9 7 5

♠ J 10 6 5 4
♡ 3
♢ 7 6 4
♣ K Q J 3

♠ Q 7
♡ 10 9 7 6 4
♢ 5 2
♣ A 8 4 2

♠ K 9
♡ A Q 8 5 2
♢ Q J 10 9 8
♣ 6

Playing in six diamonds, South ruffed the second club and drew three rounds of trumps, East discarding a club. Two hearts were cashed, a club was ruffed by declarer's last trump, and this was the end position:

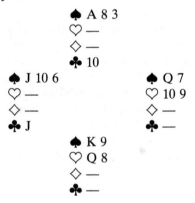

♠ A 8 3
♡ —
♢ —
♣ 10

♠ J 10 6
♡ —
♢ —
♣ J

♠ Q 7
♡ 10 9
♢ —
♣ —

♠ K 9
♡ Q 8
♢ —
♣ —

On the queen of hearts West was squeezed. It was a mistake, you see, for East to throw a club on the third round of trumps. He should have thrown a spade, protecting partner from the eventual squeeze. Early discards are often critical.

Reversing the Trend

Dealer South   Game all

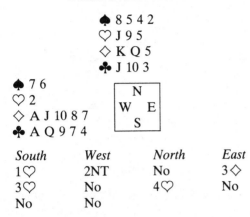

```
              ♠ 8 5 4 2
              ♡ J 9 5
              ◇ K Q 5
              ♣ J 10 3
♠ 7 6              ┌─────┐
♡ 2               │  N  │
◇ A J 10 8 7      │W   E│
♣ A Q 9 7 4       │  S  │
                  └─────┘
```

South	West	North	East
1♡	2NT	No	3◇
3♡	No	4♡	No
No	No		

I am not, myself, in favour of these jumps to 2NT on moderate hands; far more often than not, all they do is help the opponents to judge where the cards lie.

However, I show the bidding as it occurred at the table. From West's angle, the best hope of defeating the contract was to find partner with a shortage in clubs, so he began with the ace of clubs. Partner plays the 6, declarer the 5. What now?

Answer 26

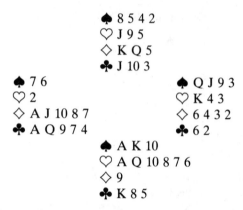

```
                    ♠ 8 5 4 2
                    ♡ J 9 5
                    ◇ K Q 5
                    ♣ J 10 3
    ♠ 7 6                              ♠ Q J 9 3
    ♡ 2                                ♡ K 4 3
    ◇ A J 10 8 7                       ◇ 6 4 3 2
    ♣ A Q 9 7 4                        ♣ 6 2
                    ♠ A K 10
                    ♡ A Q 10 8 7 6
                    ◇ 9
                    ♣ K 8 5
```

South plays in four hearts after West has overcalled with 2NT and East has bid three diamonds. West begins with the ace of clubs, on which East plays the 6 and declarer the 5.

The best chance must be to find partner with a doubleton club. To deny dummy an entry, West must continue with the queen of clubs. South wins and will probably lead his singleton diamond. West goes up with the ace and leads a third club, for his partner to ruff. Now East has a safe exit in the queen of spades and must make another trick with the king of hearts.

Reversing the trend, East–West have actually benefited from the 2NT overcall; if they found the right defence, that is.

27   **Special Selection**

Dealer South . Game all

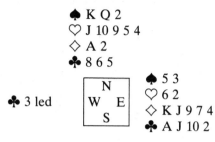

♠ K Q 2
♡ J 10 9 5 4
◇ A 2
♣ 8 6 5

♣ 3 led

♠ 5 3
♡ 6 2
◇ K J 9 7 4
♣ A J 10 2

South	West	North	East
1♠	No	2♡	No
3♡	No	3♠	No
4♠	No	No	No

West leads the 3 of clubs. You win with the ace and return the jack, on which South plays the queen and West the king. A third club is ruffed. South draws trumps, plays ace and queen of hearts, losing to the king, and claims the contract.

'Why didn't you lead a diamond after the second club?' East demanded.

West's hand was:

♠ 7 6 4
♡ K 8 3
◇ 10 6 5
♣ K 9 7 3

Who should take the blame, and why?

Answer 27

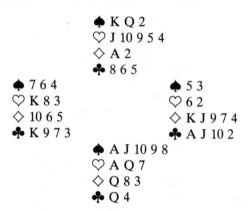

```
              ♠ K Q 2
              ♡ J 10 9 5 4
              ◇ A 2
              ♣ 8 6 5
  ♠ 7 6 4                      ♠ 5 3
  ♡ K 8 3                      ♡ 6 2
  ◇ 10 6 5                     ◇ K J 9 7 4
  ♣ K 9 7 3                    ♣ A J 10 2
              ♠ A J 10 9 8
              ♡ A Q 7
              ◇ Q 8 3
              ♣ Q 4
```

Defending against four hearts, West leads a low club to the ace, a return of the jack is covered by the queen and king, and West tries a third round. Alas! South ruffs, draws trumps, and makes his contract after giving up a trick to the king of hearts.

'Why didn't you lead a diamond after the second round of trumps?' East wanted to know.

Could West be sure? From his point of view, East might have held just three clubs, A J 10, and it might have been essential to cash these tricks immediately (for example, if South had held ◇ K J x).

Was there anything East could have done to show that he wanted a diamond switch after two rounds of clubs? Yes, he might have thought of returning the *ten* of clubs at trick two. Then West would not be tempted to lead a third round of clubs.

28   **Summer Comes Early**

Dealer North   Game all

```
                    ♠ A K J 3 2
                    ♡ 9 4 2
                    ◇ K 3
                    ♣ A K 5
    ♠ 10 9 7        ┌─────────┐
    ♡ A Q J 10 8    │    N    │
    ◇ J 10          │  W   E  │
    ♣ Q J 9         │    S    │
                    └─────────┘
```

South	West	North	East
—	—	1♠	No
2♡	No	4♡	No
No	dble	No	No
No			

When North raised to four hearts West reflected that summer had come early this year.

What about the lead? Remember, you haven't had a sight of the dummy. This problem is different from others in the book, but it has its amusing side.

Answer 28

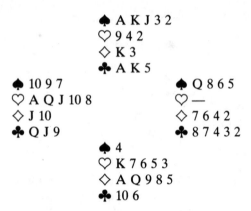

♠ A K J 3 2
♡ 9 4 2
◇ K 3
♣ A K 5

♠ 10 9 7   ♠ Q 8 6 5
♡ A Q J 10 8   ♡ —
◇ J 10   ◇ 7 6 4 2
♣ Q J 9   ♣ 8 7 4 3 2

♠ 4
♡ K 7 6 5 3
◇ A Q 9 8 5
♣ 10 6

North opened one spade, South responded two hearts, and since this response normally promises five trumps North raised to game. West doubled happily and led the jack of diamonds.

Now South was able to reduce to:

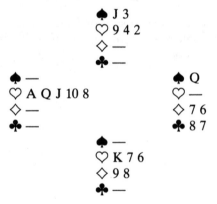

♠ J 3
♡ 9 4 2
◇ —
♣ —

♠ —   ♠ Q
♡ A Q J 10 8   ♡ —
◇ —   ◇ 7 6
♣ —   ♣ 8 7

♠ —
♡ K 7 6
◇ 9 8
♣ —

When South led a diamond West was able to score his honours but little else.

It was, of course, a calamitous error not to begin with ace and queen of trumps.

Twelve On Top?

Dealer North   Love all

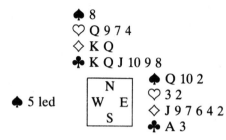

♠ 8
♡ Q 9 7 4
♦ K Q
♣ K Q J 10 9 8

♠ Q 10 2
♡ 3 2
♦ J 9 7 6 4 2
♣ A 3

♠ 5 led

South	West	North	East
—	—	1♣	No
2♦	No	3♣	No
3♡	No	4♡	No
4NT	No	5♣	No
6NT	No	No	No

Partner's lead of the 5 of spades runs to the queen and ace. On the first round of clubs your partner plays the 2 and you hold up. On the next round West plays the club 5. What do you lead now?

Answer 29

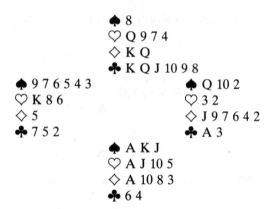

```
                    ♠ 8
                    ♡ Q 9 7 4
                    ◇ K Q
                    ♣ K Q J 10 9 8
    ♠ 9 7 6 5 4 3              ♠ Q 10 2
    ♡ K 8 6                    ♡ 3 2
    ◇ 5                        ◇ J 9 7 6 4 2
    ♣ 7 5 2                    ♣ A 3
                    ♠ A K J
                    ♡ A J 10 5
                    ◇ A 10 8 3
                    ♣ 6 4
```

West's lead of the 5 of spades is somewhat old-fashioned – second from the top is now normal from bad suits – but the lead of fourth best sometimes helps partner to obtain a count.

You win the second round of clubs and perhaps your finger is on the 10 of spades? Take it off! South certainly holds the king of spades (why otherwise has he elected to play in notrumps?) and quite possibly the jack as well. If he has A K of hearts and ace of diamonds there will be no defence, but perhaps he is missing the king of hearts and did not know which way to go over the raise to four hearts. If this is the case, you can take advantage of the block in diamonds. Return a heart now, not a spade. South will still have twelve tricks on top, but there will be no way to enjoy them all.

30   **Welcome Find**

Dealer South   Love all

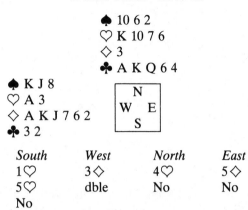

♠ 10 6 2
♡ K 10 7 6
♢ 3
♣ A K Q 6 4

♠ K J 8
♡ A 3
♢ A K J 7 6 2
♣ 3 2

South	West	North	East
1♡	3♢	4♡	5♢
5♡	dble	No	No
No			

Not a supporter of weak jump overcalls, West preferred a strong jump overcall to a take-out double. Happy to have forced his opponents to the five level, he led the ace of diamonds, on which his partner plays the 4 and declarer the 5. Two tricks were in sight. Where should he go for the third trick?

Answer 30

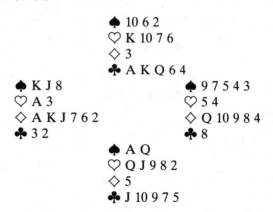

```
              ♠ 10 6 2
              ♡ K 10 7 6
              ◇ 3
              ♣ A K Q 6 4
♠ K J 8                        ♠ 9 7 5 4 3
♡ A 3                          ♡ 5 4
◇ A K J 7 6 2                  ◇ Q 10 9 8 4
♣ 3 2                          ♣ 8
              ♠ A Q
              ♡ Q J 9 8 2
              ◇ 5
              ♣ J 10 9 7 5
```

South played in five hearts doubled after West had made a jump overcall in diamonds and had been supported by his partner.

After the ace of diamonds had held the first trick West tried a low spade. Most players would have done the same, but there was very little chance of finding his partner with the queen of spades.

'It was difficult to place you with a singleton club and two trumps,' West said afterwards. 'It didn't occur to me to lead a club at trick two.'

'I don't know why not,' his partner replied. 'Ace and another heart gets them one down unless South can throw all his spade losers on dummy's clubs. You might as well lead a club and play for two down.'

31   **Why Wait?**

Dealer West   N–S vulnerable

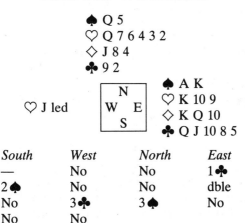

♠ Q 5
♡ Q 7 6 4 3 2
♢ J 8 4
♣ 9 2

♡ J led

♠ A K
♡ K 10 9
♢ K Q 10
♣ Q J 10 8 5

South	West	North	East
—	No	No	1♣
2♠	No	No	dble
No	3♣	3♠	No
No	No		

West's lead of the jack of hearts ran to the declarer's ace, and South led a low trump to the queen and king. East decided to cash the ace of spades and lead the queen of clubs, awaiting developments. Was this good play? If not, why not?

Answer 31

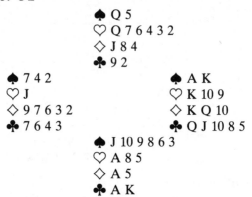

♠ Q 5
♡ Q 7 6 4 3 2
◇ J 8 4
♣ 9 2

♠ 7 4 2
♡ J
◇ 9 7 6 3 2
♣ 7 6 4 3

♠ A K
♡ K 10 9
◇ K Q 10
♣ Q J 10 8 5

♠ J 10 9 8 6 3
♡ A 8 5
◇ A 5
♣ A K

South plays in three spades after East has opened one club. The jack of hearts runs to the ace. East wins two trump tricks and then leads ♣ Q. South runs four more trumps, arriving at this position:

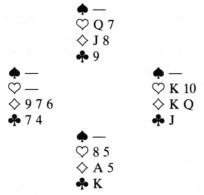

♠ —
♡ Q 7
◇ J 8
♣ 9

♠ —
♡ —
◇ 9 7 6
♣ 7 4

♠ —
♡ K 10
◇ K Q
♣ J

♠ —
♡ 8 5
◇ A 5
♣ K

South cashes ♣ K and exits with ace and another diamond, forcing East to concede a trick to dummy's queen of hearts.

When in with ♠ K East should have played ♡ K. As the cards lie, he can give his partner a ruff and will make a diamond trick later. West might have led from a doubleton heart, but what matter? Since dummy has no entry, East can simply cash ♠ A and wait for a diamond trick.

Part II

Deals 32–65

32 **A Push**

Dealer East   Love all

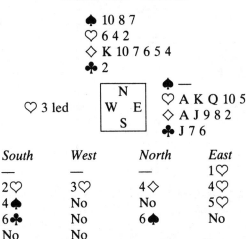

♠ 10 8 7
♡ 6 4 2
♢ K 10 7 6 5 4
♣ 2

♡ 3 led

♠ —
♡ A K Q 10 5
♢ A J 9 8 2
♣ J 7 6

South	West	North	East
—	—	—	1♡
2♡	3♡	4♢	4♡
4♠	No	No	5♡
6♣	No	6♠	No
No	No		

At poker a 'push' means that two hands are exactly equal and no money passes. Here East tried a different kind of push and was not too happy when South, whom he knew to be a resourceful player, allowed himself to be driven into six spades.

West led the 3 of hearts. Have you a defensive plan of any sort? There are two possibilities, one rather better than the other.

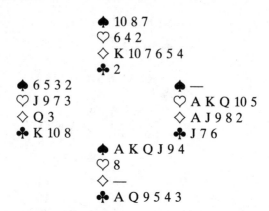

♠ 10 8 7
♡ 6 4 2
◇ K 10 7 6 5 4
♣ 2

♠ 6 5 3 2
♡ J 9 7 3
◇ Q 3
♣ K 10 8

♠ —
♡ A K Q 10 5
◇ A J 9 8 2
♣ J 7 6

♠ A K Q J 9 4
♡ 8
◇ —
♣ A Q 9 5 4 3

After East has opened the bidding, South allows himself to be pushed into six spades. West leads a low heart.

From the defenders' point of view, the sight of the dummy, with the singleton club and useful spades, is alarming. South can be counted for a singleton heart after the lead of ♡ 3, but where will the next trick come from? If South is 6–1–0–6, as seems likely, he will be able to stand a heart return.

One idea is to try a low diamond at trick two. South might possibly ruff and later finesse in clubs. But South will be suspicious in view of East's energetic bidding.

There is a cleverer plan: win the first heart with the *ace* and return the 5. If this gives declarer the impression that East's hearts are only A Q 10 x x, he *may* decide that the club finesse must be right; and he *may* cross to dummy with a trump; intending to finesse the queen of clubs. When the trumps break 4–0 the hand becomes unmanageable.

Beginners, Too

Dealer East   E–W vulnerable

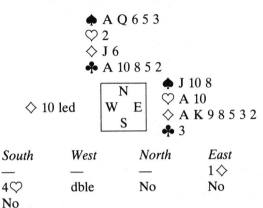

♠ A Q 6 5 3
♡ 2
◇ J 6
♣ A 10 8 5 2

♠ J 10 8
♡ A 10
◇ A K 9 8 5 3 2
♣ 3

◇ 10 led

South	West	North	East
—	—	—	1◇
4♡	dble	No	No
No			

West leads the 10 of diamonds and all follow to the ace and king. What should East play now? A trump promotion will work in time if West has J x of hearts or 9 x x. Is that the best chance?

Answer 33

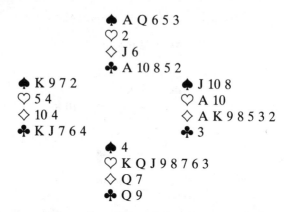

```
              ♠ A Q 6 5 3
              ♡ 2
              ◇ J 6
              ♣ A 10 8 5 2
♠ K 9 7 2                      ♠ J 10 8
♡ 5 4                          ♡ A 10
◇ 10 4                         ◇ A K 9 8 5 3 2
♣ K J 7 6 4                    ♣ 3
              ♠ 4
              ♡ K Q J 9 8 7 6 3
              ◇ Q 7
              ♣ Q 9
```

East opened one diamond and South overcalled with four hearts, which was doubled by West. The defence made the first two tricks in diamonds. Seeing nothing better, East led a third diamond. South ruffed high, finessed the queen of spades and led a heart from dummy. The rest of the play presented no problem.

The trump promotion was a very long shot because South had bid four hearts without an ace in his hand and surely had very good trumps.

East missed a better chance. Like a beginner who cashes his top winners and then looks round, he should have followed ace-king of diamonds with ace of hearts and then a club to the 9, jack and ace. Now the luckless declarer is unable to return to hand for a spade finesse.

Chance for Folly

Dealer South   E–W vulnerable

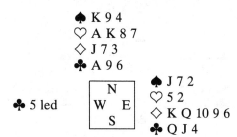

♠ K 9 4
♥ A K 8 7
♦ J 7 3
♣ A 9 6

♣ 5 led

♠ J 7 2
♥ 5 2
♦ K Q 10 9 6
♣ Q J 4

South opens with a weak two hearts and North raises to game. West leads the 5 of clubs and you win with the jack, South playing the 2.

Already it is possible to do something foolish. Such as?

Answer 34

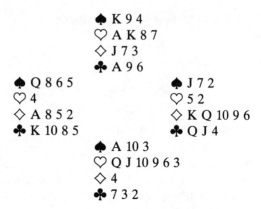

♠ K 9 4
♡ A K 8 7
♢ J 7 3
♣ A 9 6

♠ Q 8 6 5
♡ 4
♢ A 8 5 2
♣ K 10 8 5

♠ J 7 2
♡ 5 2
♢ K Q 10 9 6
♣ Q J 4

♠ A 10 3
♡ Q J 10 9 6 3
♢ 4
♣ 7 3 2

South opens with a weak two hearts and North raises to four hearts. West leads a low club and the jack holds the first trick.

Perhaps it is slightly tempting to give partner a picture of the diamond situation by laying down the king. But you see what this leads to? South soon reduces to this situation:

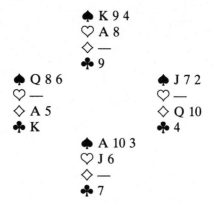

♠ K 9 4
♡ A 8
♢ —
♣ 9

♠ Q 8 6
♡ —
♢ A 5
♣ K

♠ J 7 2
♡ —
♢ Q 10
♣ 4

♠ A 10 3
♡ J 6
♢ —
♣ 7

South exits with a club and plays for divided honours in spades. To make sure you don't run short of exit cards, you must continue clubs at trick two, not lay down the king of diamonds.

35

Delayed Action

Dealer West   Game all

```
                ♠ 10
                ♡ K 10 9 6 3
                ◇ 7 5 4
                ♣ Q J 9 3
  ♠ 9 8 5          ┌─────┐
  ♡ Q 7 2          │  N  │
  ◇ A Q J 3        │W   E│
  ♣ 10 8 4         │  S  │
                   └─────┘
```

South	West	North	East
—	No	No	No
1♠	No	1NT	No
2♠	No	No	No

With no very attractive lead, West began with the 9 of spades.
East won with the ace and returned the 9 of diamonds, which
South covered with the 10. West won and exited with a trump.
After drawing a third round of trumps South led a low heart to
the 9 and ace. The defence made two more tricks in diamonds,
but declarer then crossed to the king of hearts, finessed the queen
of clubs, and just made his contract.

A couple of hands later East said thoughtfully: 'You remember that hand we defended in two spades? I think we could have
beaten it.'

What did East mean?

Answer 35

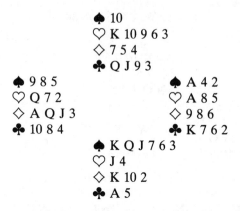

♠ 10
♡ K 10 9 6 3
♢ 7 5 4
♣ Q J 9 3

♠ 9 8 5
♡ Q 7 2
♢ A Q J 3
♣ 10 8 4

♠ A 4 2
♡ A 8 5
♢ 9 8 6
♣ K 7 6 2

♠ K Q J 7 6 3
♡ J 4
♢ K 10 2
♣ A 5

South opened one spade after three passes and became declarer in two spades. West led a trump, East won with the ace and returned ♢ 9, which was covered by the 10 and jack. West exited with another trump. After drawing a third round South led a low heart to the 10 and ace. The defence took two more diamonds, but that was all.

South's lead of a low heart was well judged. If he leads the jack both defenders will play low and after the next heart and two more diamonds West will exit with the fourth diamond.

As the play went, West missed the blocking play of the queen of hearts on the first round. East heads the king with the ace and returns a diamond. There is no entry to dummy and South is never able to take the club finesse.

36

Diamond Cutting

Dealer South   Game all

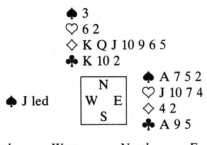

```
                ♠ 3
                ♡ 6 2
                ◇ K Q J 10 9 6 5
                ♣ K 10 2
                                    ♠ A 7 5 2
                          N         ♡ J 10 7 4
      ♠ J led        W    E         ◇ 4 2
                          S         ♣ A 9 5
```

South	West	North	East
1♡	No	2◇	No
2♠	No	3◇	No
3NT	No	No	No

Your partner leads the jack of spades. What is your general plan of defence? Do you play the ace and return a spade? Do you win and switch? Or do you play low on the spade lead, which is probably from J 10 9 x?

Answer 36

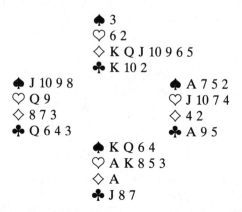

```
              ♠ 3
              ♡ 6 2
              ◇ K Q J 10 9 6 5
              ♣ K 10 2
♠ J 10 9 8                    ♠ A 7 5 2
♡ Q 9                         ♡ J 10 7 4
◇ 8 7 3                       ◇ 4 2
♣ Q 6 4 3                     ♣ A 9 5
              ♠ K Q 6 4
              ♡ A K 8 5 3
              ◇ A
              ♣ J 8 7
```

South, who has bid hearts and spades, plays in 3NT, and West leads the jack of spades.

How are you going to beat this hand? South, who has reversed, must certainly hold one of the minor suit aces. If he has Q J x of clubs and at least one diamond, there is nothing you can do. The only chance, really, is that he has a singleton ace of diamonds and nothing very much in clubs.

Having reached this conclusion, you must take the ace of spades and try to force out the king of clubs by leading the 5. As the cards lie, the 7 of clubs is covered by the queen and king, and it is easy then to duck the next club and kill the dummy.

Note that this defence would probably work if South held ♣ Q x x instead of J x x. It's not likely that South would play the queen and finesse the 10 on the next round.

Early Error

Dealer North   Game all

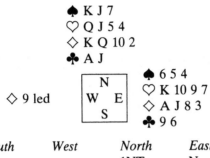

♠ K J 7
♡ Q J 5 4
◇ K Q 10 2
♣ A J

♠ 6 5 4
♡ K 10 9 7
◇ A J 8 3
♣ 9 6

◇ 9 led

South	West	North	East
—	—	1NT	No
3♠	No	4♣	No
4♡	No	4♠	No
5♣	No	6♠	No
No	No		

North has not a great hand for his vulnerable notrump, but it is normal, when partner forces, to show aces below game level.

At the table West's lead of ◇ 9 was covered by the queen and ace. East returned a trump at trick two. South drew trumps, West discarding a club on the third round, then led the queen of hearts from dummy. East covered and was in bad trouble when South played three top clubs, followed by a fourth spade.

The main question is: Did East make a mistake? If so, what was it?

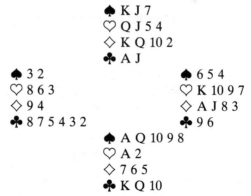

♠ K J 7
♥ Q J 5 4
♦ K Q 10 2
♣ A J

♠ 3 2   ♠ 6 5 4
♥ 8 6 3   ♥ K 10 9 7
♦ 9 4   ♦ A J 8 3
♣ 8 7 5 4 3 2   ♣ 9 6

♠ A Q 10 9 8
♥ A 2
♦ 7 6 5
♣ K Q 10

North–South played in six spades. West led ♦ 9 which was covered by the queen and ace. A trump was returned, and after three rounds of trumps the queen of hearts was led and covered. After three clubs and a fourth spade the position was:

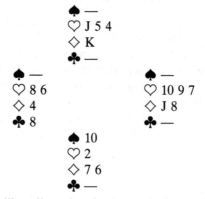

♠ —
♥ J 5 4
♦ K
♣ —

♠ —   ♠ —
♥ 8 6   ♥ 10 9 7
♦ 4   ♦ J 8
♣ 8   ♣ —

♠ 10
♥ 2
♦ 7 6
♣ —

East had still to discard and was caught in a ruffing squeeze.

If East had declined to cover ♥ Q earlier on, there would have been a criss-cross squeeze in the red suits.

The mistake occurred on the first trick when East covered the queen of diamonds with the ace. It is almost always better to keep major tenaces, A J, than minor tenaces, J x against K 10.

38 **Four Into Three**

Dealer North   Game all

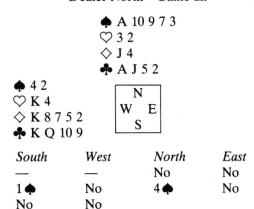

♠ A 10 9 7 3
♡ 3 2
◇ J 4
♣ A J 5 2

♠ 4 2
♡ K 4
◇ K 8 7 5 2
♣ K Q 10 9

South	West	North	East
—	—	No	No
1♠	No	4♠	No
No	No		

You lead the king of clubs, dummy wins, and partner plays the 3. South now leads a low diamond from dummy: 6 from East, 10 from declarer, and you win with the king.

What is going on, do you think? What do you do now?

Answer 38

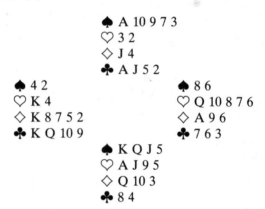

♠ A 10 9 7 3
♡ 3 2
♢ J 4
♣ A J 5 2

♠ 4 2
♡ K 4
♢ K 8 7 5 2
♣ K Q 10 9

♠ 8 6
♡ Q 10 8 7 6
♢ A 9 6
♣ 7 6 3

♠ K Q J 5
♡ A J 9 5
♢ Q 10 3
♣ 8 4

South opened one spade in third position and North raised to four spades. West led the king of clubs, dummy won, and East played the 3. Then a low diamond went to the 10 and king.

West could judge the club distribution from his partner's play of the 3 on the first trick. The diamonds were not so easy to read – South might have held A 10 9 or Q 10 x. In any case, it looked as though he was planning to establish a diamond for the discard of a heart from dummy.

Having reached this conclusion, West laid down the king of hearts. East played the 7 and South false-carded with the 9. West then led a second heart, enabling the declarer to discard a diamond from dummy and make the contract, losing one trick in each of the side suits.

'You should have given me your lowest heart,' said West. 'I thought you had the ace of hearts and that we'd make a trick in clubs.'

The deal occurred in a French international trial, and Pierre Schemeil made the point that West could have made a better play himself. He should have led a low heart, not the king. The queen loses to the ace, but the defenders will surely take three more tricks.

39

Funny But True

Dealer South   Love all

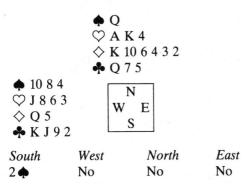

♠ Q
♡ A K 4
◇ K 10 6 4 3 2
♣ Q 7 5

♠ 10 8 4
♡ J 8 6 3
◇ Q 5
♣ K J 9 2

South	West	North	East
2♠	No	No	No

South opened with a weak two spades and all passed. West made the attacking lead of the queen of diamonds, which ran to the declarer's ace. South returned a diamond, perhaps intending to finesse the 10 and discard a loser on the king, but he changed his mind and went up with the king from dummy. The queen of spades was covered by the king and ace, and South led back a low spade.

As West, have you any special defensive plan?

Answer 39

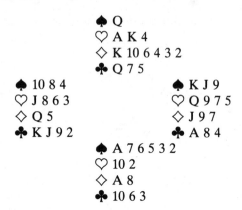

```
              ♠ Q
              ♡ A K 4
              ◇ K 10 6 4 3 2
              ♣ Q 7 5
  ♠ 10 8 4                    ♠ K J 9
  ♡ J 8 6 3                   ♡ Q 9 7 5
  ◇ Q 5                       ◇ J 9 7
  ♣ K J 9 2                   ♣ A 8 4
              ♠ A 7 6 5 3 2
              ♡ 10 2
              ◇ A 8
              ♣ 10 6 3
```

South opened with a weak two spades – not my idea of a two-bid, but common enough in pairs events. All passed and West led the queen of diamonds, which ran to the ace.

South returned a diamond, presumably intending to finesse, but he changed his mind and went up with the king. The queen of spades was covered by the king and ace, and the next spade was won by East's 9. If East plays the jack of diamonds at this point, South can discard a club. He loses, in effect, two spades, two clubs and a diamond.

'Were your spades the K J 9?' asked West. 'Damn, we could have beaten it. I must go in with the 10 of spades and switch to the jack of clubs. You ruff the fourth club with the jack of spades and I make my 8. Funny, we always beat it if your spades are K J x instead of K J 9.'

Yes, and there are other possibilities, too. For example, if West's spades are 10 7 x and declarer's A 9 x x x x, the 10 of spades is necessary and the 7 is later promoted.

40

Gallant Try

Dealer West   N–S vulnerable

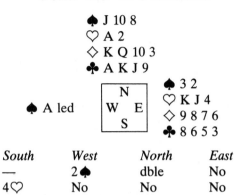

♠ J 10 8
♡ A 2
♢ K Q 10 3
♣ A K J 9

♠ 3 2
♡ K J 4
♢ 9 8 7 6
♣ 8 6 5 3

♠ A led

South	West	North	East
—	2♠	dble	No
4♡	No	No	No

Your partner, who has opened with a weak two-bid, begins with ace, king and queen of spades. What will you play on the third round?

Answer 40

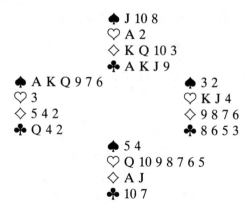

```
              ♠ J 10 8
              ♡ A 2
              ◇ K Q 10 3
              ♣ A K J 9
♠ A K Q 9 7 6              ♠ 3 2
♡ 3                        ♡ K J 4
◇ 5 4 2                    ◇ 9 8 7 6
♣ Q 4 2                    ♣ 8 6 5 3
              ♠ 5 4
              ♡ Q 10 9 8 7 6 5
              ◇ A J
              ♣ 10 7
```

South plays in four hearts after West has opened with a weak two spades. West begins with three top spades. The question is, what do you do on the third round?

At the table you would no doubt throw a club and surrender the contract when South led a heart to the ace and returned a heart.

There is, however, one small chance to upset the applecart. Suppose you ruff with the *king* of hearts. It is just possible that South will play for the possibility of this being a singleton king; he may run the 10 of hearts when he gains the lead.

41　Hollow Sound

Dealer South　E–W vulnerable

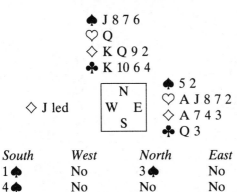

♠ J 8 7 6
♡ Q
♢ K Q 9 2
♣ K 10 6 4

♢ J led

♠ 5 2
♡ A J 8 7 2
♢ A 7 4 3
♣ Q 3

South	West	North	East
1♠	No	3♠	No
4♠	No	No	No

West's lead of the jack of diamonds is covered by the queen and ace, and South drops the 6. What do you play at trick two, and why?

Answer 41

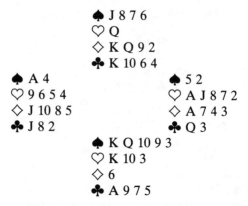

```
              ♠ J 8 7 6
              ♡ Q
              ◇ K Q 9 2
              ♣ K 10 6 4
♠ A 4                        ♠ 5 2
♡ 9 6 5 4                    ♡ A J 8 7 2
◇ J 10 8 5                   ◇ A 7 4 3
♣ J 8 2                      ♣ Q 3
              ♠ K Q 10 9 3
              ♡ K 10 3
              ◇ 6
              ♣ A 9 7 5
```

South is in four spades and West's lead of the jack of diamonds is covered by the queen and ace.

In a pairs event the play was much the same at several tables. East returned an innocuous trump and West played a second round. South played a low heart to the queen and ace, and East found himself end-played. Neither a heart nor a diamond nor a club advances his cause.

East might say to his partner, 'Why didn't you lead a heart when you were in with the ace of spades?' but the rebuke has a hollow sound. It was for East to cash the ace of hearts at trick two. There can be no advantage in retaining this card.

42   If Not, Why Not?

Dealer South   Game all

```
                    ♠ J 7 6
                    ♡ A K 3 2
                    ◇ A 10 9 7 6
                    ♣ 2
    ♠ 2              ┌─────────┐
    ♡ Q J 9          │    N    │
    ◇ 5 3 2          │  W   E  │
    ♣ A K J 9 7 6    │    S    │
                     └─────────┘
```

South	West	North	East
4♠	No	5♠	No
6♠	No	No	No

North's five spades was a good choice: it showed that he did not possess two losers in any of the side suits.

You lead a top club and partner plays the 3, declarer the 5. The likelihood here is that partner is showing an odd number. If he has three clubs there will be no defence. You assume that he has five and South a singleton.

What would you lead at trick two? The queen of hearts looks so obvious that you will hardly believe this could be right. We will put the question in an unusual way, therefore: Is the queen of hearts best? If not, why not?

Answer 42

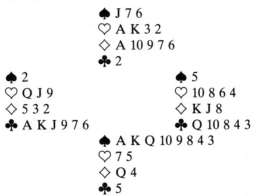

♠ J 7 6
♡ A K 3 2
♦ A 10 9 7 6
♣ 2

♠ 2
♡ Q J 9
♦ 5 3 2
♣ A K J 9 7 6

♠ 5
♡ 10 8 6 4
♦ K J 8
♣ Q 10 8 4 3

♠ A K Q 10 9 8 4 3
♡ 7 5
♦ Q 4
♣ 5

West holds the first trick with the king of clubs. What next?

It looks as though South has eleven tricks on top – eight spades and three winners in the red suits. A heart at trick two may result in a trump squeeze. This will be the ending:

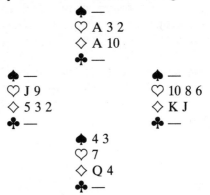

♠ —
♡ A 3 2
♦ A 10
♣ —

♠ —
♡ J 9
♦ 5 3 2
♣ —

♠ —
♡ 10 8 6
♦ K J
♣ —

♠ 4 3
♡ 7
♦ Q 4
♣ —

Dummy will discard a diamond on the 4 of spades and East will be squeezed. It is true that South might misread the situation altogether and attempt a squeeze against West, but there is no reason to take this risk. The simple way for West to look at it is this. If I lead a diamond now there cannot be a squeeze, because I can look after the hearts and he will guard the diamonds.

Killing Time

Dealer South   Game all

```
              ♠ A 8 5 3
              ♡ 3
              ♦ 10
              ♣ A Q 10 9 7 4 3
♠ K 10 9 7 6 4   ┌─────────┐
♡ Q J 10 8 7     │    N    │
♦ 2              │  W   E  │
♣ 8              │    S    │
                 └─────────┘
```

South	West	North	East
1♦	2♦	3♣	No
3NT	No	No	dble
No	No	No	

Your overcall of two diamonds is 'Michaels', signifying a major two-suiter with not enough top cards for a take-out double. I am not myself an admirer of these weak overcalls because they are very helpful to the opponents if they obtain the contract. However, on this occasion your partner has doubled, so all may turn out well.

You begin with the queen of hearts, on which East plays the 6 and declarer the 4. What is your next move?

Answer 43

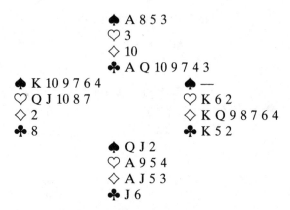

♠ A 8 5 3
♡ 3
♢ 10
♣ A Q 10 9 7 4 3

♠ K 10 9 7 6 4
♡ Q J 10 8 7
♢ 2
♣ 8

♠ —
♡ K 6 2
♢ K Q 9 8 7 6 4
♣ K 5 2

♠ Q J 2
♡ A 9 5 4
♢ A J 5 3
♣ J 6

South plays in 3NT doubled after he has opened one diamond and you have made a Michaels overcall of two diamonds, showing a limited hand with length in both majors. You lead the queen of hearts, on which East plays the 6 and declarer the 4.

Although it is likely that South has the three missing spades (since he bid 3NT), you must try the king of spades at trick two in the hope of killing the club suit. If the king of spades is allowed to hold, you must go back to hearts, leading low to East's king. If this is not taken, East will switch to the king of diamonds, ensuring five tricks for the defence.

Note that a low heart to the king at trick two is not good enough. South will hold up again and make the contract easily.

Last Word

Dealer North   E–W vulnerable

```
              ♠ 5 3 2
              ♡ A K J 5 3
              ◇ K Q 6 4 2
              ♣ —
                          ♠ K 8 7
              N           ♡ Q 10 8 7
♡ 9 led    W     E        ◇ A 5
              S           ♣ Q 10 7 3
```

South	West	North	East
—	—	1♡	No
1♠	No	2◇	No
3♣	No	3♠	No
4♠	No	5♣	No
6♠	No	No	No

West led the 9 of hearts and South won in dummy. He played a spade to the queen and then led the jack of diamonds. East let this hold – good play. A second round of diamonds went to the queen and ace.

What should East have played now? There were several possibilities.

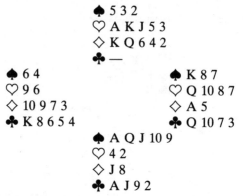

Playing in six spades, South won the heart lead, finessed
♠ Q, and led a second diamond to the queen and ace, leaving:

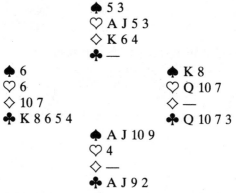

At the table East returned a low club. The 9 forced the king
and dummy ruffed. The king of diamonds was led and East did
well not to ruff. However, the rest of the spades followed and
East was squeezed.

East might have led the queen of clubs instead of the low one.
South may then win with the ace and lead the jack, transferring
the menace.

West had the last word. 'Just return a heart when you're in,'
he said to East. 'This kills the entries for any squeeze.'

45　Loose Wheel

Dealer North　N–S vulnerable

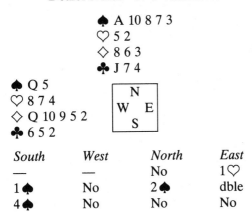

♠ A 10 8 7 3
♡ 5 2
◇ 8 6 3
♣ J 7 4

♠ Q 5
♡ 8 7 4
◇ Q 10 9 5 2
♣ 6 5 2

South	West	North	East
—	—	No	1♡
1♠	No	2♠	dble
4♠	No	No	No

West led the 8 of hearts and East cashed the queen and king, South following with the 3 and 9. East then led the 4 of diamonds, which was covered by South's jack and West's queen. A diamond return went to the king and ace.

Already a wheel had come off. When did it happen?

Answer 45

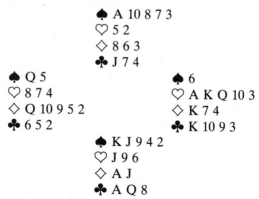

♠ A 10 8 7 3
♡ 5 2
♢ 8 6 3
♣ J 7 4

♠ Q 5
♡ 8 7 4
♢ Q 10 9 5 2
♣ 6 5 2

♠ 6
♡ A K Q 10 3
♢ K 7 4
♣ K 10 9 3

♠ K J 9 4 2
♡ J 9 6
♢ A J
♣ A Q 8

Most players, holding the South hand, would have doubled the opening one heart, but I see nothing wrong with the simple overcall.

West led the 8 of hearts against the eventual four spades. After cashing two hearts East led a low diamond to the jack and queen. West returned a diamond, and from that point the defence was lost. South drew trumps, ruffed a diamond, and played three more trumps from dummy. On the last spade East, holding a top heart and K 10 9 of clubs, was squeezed in front of the declarer.

West was mainly to blame. Since the jack of hearts had not appeared, it was clear that South held this card. West should have played a third heart to kill what later became a menace card for the squeeze.

Two other points are worth mentioning. First, South should have dropped the jack of hearts on the second round, making it a little more difficult for West to read the position. Second, as the Norwegian author, Helge Vinje, has pointed out, defenders with holdings such as A K Q x x or A K Q x x x should vary their play to indicate length; it is easy enough to play, say, queen and king, or queen and ace, according to whether an odd or even number of cards is held. The same argument applies to the opening lead from such as A K x x or A K x x x.

46

Minor Role

Dealer North   Love all

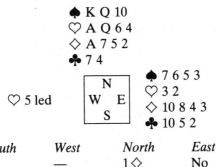

♠ K Q 10
♡ A Q 6 4
◇ A 7 5 2
♣ 7 4

♠ 7 6 5 3
♡ 3 2
◇ 10 8 4 3
♣ 10 5 2

♡ 5 led

South	West	North	East
—	—	1◇	No
1♡	dble	3♡	No
No	No		

South wins the heart lead in dummy and plays a low club to the 8 and jack. West exits with a trump and a second club runs to the 9 and queen. West now leads a third trump; you discard a spade and South wins.

Perhaps, with your very poor hand, you have been 'resting' so far? Are you sure you haven't missed a small, but possibly vital, point?

Answer 46

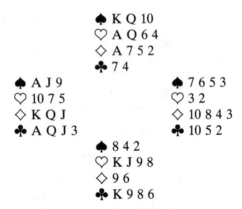

♠ K Q 10
♡ A Q 6 4
◇ A 7 5 2
♣ 7 4

♠ A J 9
♡ 10 7 5
◇ K Q J
♣ A Q J 3

♠ 7 6 5 3
♡ 3 2
◇ 10 8 4 3
♣ 10 5 2

♠ 8 4 2
♡ K J 9 8
◇ 9 6
♣ K 9 8 6

South plays in three hearts after West has made a take-out double. West leads a trump, which is won in dummy, and the declarer's first move is a club to the 8 and jack.

Perhaps it did not strike you at the time, but you had a chance to influence the course of play by following with the 5 of clubs. South wins the next heart in dummy and leads another club, on which you play the 2.

South wins the third round of hearts and has the option now of leading the 6 of clubs to bring down the ace, or the king of clubs to pin the 10. If he is the sort of player himself who is assiduous in 'giving the count', he may think that your 5 and 2 of clubs indicate four cards. In this case he will lead a low club and lose three more tricks – a spade, a club and a diamond.

If, on the other hand, you play the 2 and 5 of clubs he may follow with the king, pinning your 10. Then the 6 of clubs will be prompted and a later finesse of the 10 of spades will give him the contract.

This kind of false-carding is often effective when you have a holding such as J x x x or 10 x x in a side suit. You mustn't make it easy for the declarer to assess the distribution.

47

No Assistance

Dealer East   E–W vulnerable

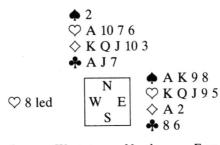

        ♠ 2
        ♡ A 10 7 6
        ◇ K Q J 10 3
        ♣ A J 7

                        ♠ A K 9 8
                        ♡ K Q J 9 5
    ♡ 8 led   ◇ A 2
                        ♣ 8 6

South	West	North	East
—	—	—	1♡
1♠	No	3NT	dble
4♣	No	4◇	No
4♠	No	No	dble
No	No	No	

South wins the heart lead in dummy, following suit himself, and a trump runs to the jack. South continues with the queen of spades, partner follows and you win.

You were fairly confident when you doubled four spades. What are you going to do now?

Answer 47

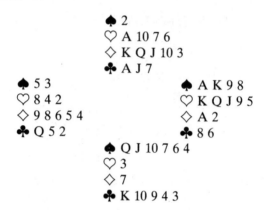

```
            ♠ 2
            ♡ A 10 7 6
            ◇ K Q J 10 3
            ♣ A J 7
♠ 5 3                       ♠ A K 9 8
♡ 8 4 2                     ♡ K Q J 9 5
◇ 9 8 6 5 4                 ◇ A 2
♣ Q 5 2                     ♣ 8 6
            ♠ Q J 10 7 6 4
            ♡ 3
            ◇ 7
            ♣ K 10 9 4 3
```

South, who has shown a moderate hand with spades and clubs, plays in four spades doubled. The heart lead is won in dummy, a trump goes to the jack and the queen of spades is taken by the king.

If South had been 6–2–0–5 he would probably have led the king of diamonds from dummy at trick two, so the likely assumption is that he is 6–1–1–5. You hope to make two more spades and a diamond, but there are certain dangers in the position. You must not give the declarer a chance to reduce his trumps by ruffing. If you do this, the sequence will be: heart ruff, diamond to king and ace, heart ruffed, 10 of clubs to the jack, ace of clubs, and winning diamonds until you decide to ruff.

On such occasions the winning defence is to play the suit that does not help the declarer to shorten his trumps. If you lead a club when in with the king of spades, and another club when in with the ace of diamonds, you prevent the trump reduction.

48   Not a Compliment

Dealer North   Love all

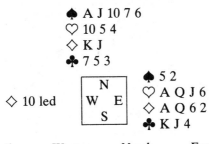

♠ A J 10 7 6
♡ 10 5 4
◇ K J
♣ 7 5 3

◇ 10 led

♠ 5 2
♡ A Q J 6
◇ A Q 6 2
♣ K J 4

South	West	North	East
		No	1♡
1♠	2♡	3♠	No
4♠	No	No	No

You hold a lot of points in the East position, but you don't propose to defend at a high level.

Your partner leads the 10 of diamonds, which seems intelligent of him, and you win the first trick with ◇ Q. You play the ace of hearts, dropping a singleton king from South. What next?

Answer 48

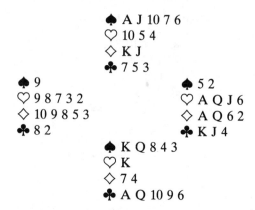

```
              ♠ A J 10 7 6
              ♡ 10 5 4
              ◇ K J
              ♣ 7 5 3
♠ 9                          ♠ 5 2
♡ 9 8 7 3 2                  ♡ A Q J 6
◇ 10 9 8 5 3                 ◇ A Q 6 2
♣ 8 2                        ♣ K J 4
              ♠ K Q 8 4 3
              ♡ K
              ◇ 7 4
              ♣ A Q 10 9 6
```

South plays in four spades after East has opened one heart and has been raised to two hearts. West leads the 10 of diamonds, which is covered by the jack and queen. East then lays down the ace of hearts, dropping the declarer's king.

It may seem natural defence now to cash the ace of diamonds and exit in hearts, hoping to pick up a club trick later. However, this can hardly gain, because if partner has the 10 of clubs the contract will surely be defeated.

There is one rather subtle chance, admittedly not easy to see at the table. If you exit with a heart, not cashing the ace of diamonds, South will ruff, play a trump to dummy, and ruff the last heart. There is a good chance then that he will later finesse the queen of clubs, cash the ace, and exit in diamonds, hoping that you began with 2–5–4–2 distribution and will have to give him a ruff-and-discard.

It is true that this line of play would be no great compliment to your play, because with the distribution he is assuming you would surely have cashed the ace of diamonds. But there it is, players often don't think of such things.

49   Not Such an Easy Discard

Dealer South   Game all

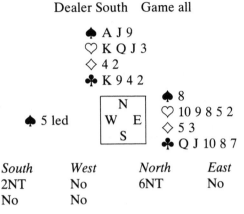

♠ A J 9
♡ K Q J 3
◇ 4 2
♣ K 9 4 2

♠ 5 led

♠ 8
♡ 10 9 8 5 2
◇ 5 3
♣ Q J 10 8 7

South	West	North	East
2NT	No	6NT	No
No	No		

It is surprising, really, that players who never fail to introduce the old Stayman when they are looking for game often decline the convention when they have enough for slam. This is foolish, because to make game in a suit you need to make ten tricks as against nine for 3NT. At slam level it is twelve tricks in either contract, so there is much more point in seeking for the 4–4 fit that may bring in an extra trick. Thus it is easy, on this occasion, to construct hands for South that would be safer in six hearts than 6NT.

However, that is by the way, because South did not hold four cards in either major. On West's lead of the 5 of spades dummy plays the 9, you follow with the 8, and South wins with the queen. To clarify the spade position he returns a spade to the jack. Now it may not seem to matter whether you discard a heart, a diamond or a club. Which would you choose, and can you say why?

111

Answer 49

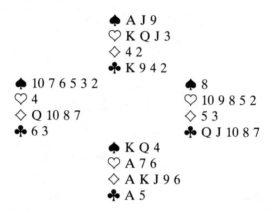

♠ A J 9
♡ K Q J 3
◇ 4 2
♣ K 9 4 2

♠ 10 7 6 5 3 2
♡ 4
◇ Q 10 8 7
♣ 6 3

♠ 8
♡ 10 9 8 5 2
◇ 5 3
♣ Q J 10 8 7

♠ K Q 4
♡ A 7 6
◇ A K J 9 6
♣ A 5

West leads a low spade against 6NT, and having noted East's 8 the declarer plays a second round of spades. East has to find a discard.

Most players, no doubt, would discard the queen of clubs, thinking 'This will tell partner, if he has a doubleton, that it will be perfectly safe for him to discard a club at any time.'

Sometimes that is a sensible sort of argument, but here the club discard is disastrous. It marks you with five or more clubs, and when you turn up with five hearts the declarer will play for an ending where he holds ♠ K and ◇ A K J 9. If West has come down to a singleton spade, South will cash the ace of spades and end-play West in diamonds. And clearly it will not help West to keep two spades and only three diamonds.

To discard a diamond on the East hand might be a mistake in some circumstances, as the distribution of the suit would then be shown up on the second round. The best discard is a heart. South will take four rounds of hearts, but he won't know how the minor suits are distributed. His next play, probably, will be a diamond finesse, and he will lose another trick at the finish.

Oddly Enough

Dealer South   Game all

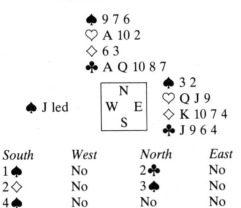

♠ 9 7 6
♡ A 10 2
◇ 6 3
♣ A Q 10 8 7

♠ J led

    ♠ 3 2
    ♡ Q J 9
    ◇ K 10 7 4
    ♣ J 9 6 4

South	West	North	East
South	*West*	*North*	*East*
1♠	No	2♣	No
2◇	No	3♠	No
4♠	No	No	No

West leads the jack of spades. South wins with the ace and leads a club to the 10 and jack. What do you play now?

Answer 50

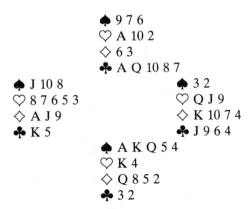

```
            ♠ 9 7 6
            ♡ A 10 2
            ◇ 6 3
            ♣ A Q 10 8 7
♠ J 10 8                    ♠ 3 2
♡ 8 7 6 5 3                 ♡ Q J 9
◇ A J 9                     ◇ K 10 7 4
♣ K 5                      ♣ J 9 6 4
            ♠ A K Q 5 4
            ♡ K 4
            ◇ Q 8 5 2
            ♣ 3 2
```

South plays in four spades after bidding spades and diamonds. West leads the jack of spades to the declarer's ace.

Needing to take care of his diamonds, South decides to play on dummy's clubs. Rightly or wrongly, he begins with a low club to the 10 and jack.

From East's point of view, this play makes sense only on the assumption that South has losing diamonds. In this case he must hold the king of hearts and his likely distribution is 5–2–4–2.

Neither a heart nor a spade return will achieve anything: South will draw trumps, then lead a club, on which partner's king will appear. Declarer will make ten tricks by way of five spades, two hearts and three clubs.

Oddly enough, a club return destroys the declarer's plan. As he has not drawn trumps yet, he cannot afford to ruff the third club with a high spade and will not be able to establish a tenth trick.

51   Offer the Chance

Dealer South   Game all

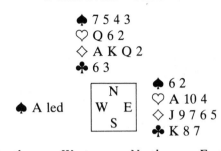

♠ 7 5 4 3
♡ Q 6 2
◇ A K Q 2
♣ 6 3

♠ 6 2
♡ A 10 4
◇ J 9 7 6 5
♣ K 8 7

♠ A led

South	West	North	East
1♣	2♣	dble	2♡
3♣	3♡	No	No
4♣	No	No	No

West's two clubs is 'Michaels', showing length in both majors.

Partner begins with ace and king of spades. You play high-low, but evidently he has five spades, since he now switches to the 5 of hearts, on which dummy plays low. What is your defensive plan now?

Answer 51

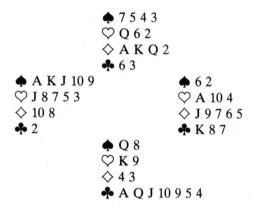

♠ 7 5 4 3
♡ Q 6 2
◇ A K Q 2
♣ 6 3

♠ A K J 10 9
♡ J 8 7 5 3
◇ 10 8
♣ 2

♠ 6 2
♡ A 10 4
◇ J 9 7 6 5
♣ K 8 7

♠ Q 8
♡ K 9
◇ 4 3
♣ A Q J 10 9 5 4

South plays in four clubs after West has made a Michaels over-call, indicating length in both majors. West cashes two top spades, then switches to the 5 of hearts, on which dummy plays low.

Looking at the diagram, you may wonder what difference it can make whether East plays the ace of hearts or the 10. Declarer has ten easy tricks either way.

That is true, in a sense, but giving an opponent a chance to go wrong is a very important part of the game. There is a good reason here for inserting the 10 of hearts. A great number of players in the South position would win with the king and try hastily to discard the second heart on the third round of diamonds. This would not be good play, in view of the bidding, but you must give him the chance.

One Way to Game

Dealer West   E–W vulnerable

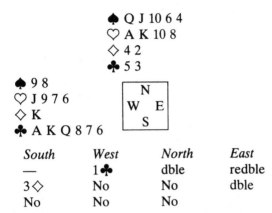

♠ Q J 10 6 4
♡ A K 10 8
♢ 4 2
♣ 5 3

♠ 9 8
♡ J 9 7 6
♢ K
♣ A K Q 8 7 6

South	West	North	East
—	1♣	dble	redble
3♢	No	No	dble
No	No	No	

Most players would prefer a simple overcall on the North hand, or a conventional move to indicate a moderate major two-suiter.

Sitting West, you begin with the ace of clubs, on which partner plays the 4 and declarer the 10. You judge that partner has played the 4 from an even number, probably four cards. What is your next move?

Answer 52

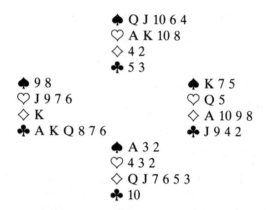

♠ Q J 10 6 4
♥ A K 10 8
⋄ 4 2
♣ 5 3

♠ 9 8
♥ J 9 7 6
⋄ K
♣ A K Q 8 7 6

♠ K 7 5
♥ Q 5
⋄ A 10 9 8
♣ J 9 4 2

♠ A 3 2
♥ 4 3 2
⋄ Q J 7 6 5 3
♣ 10

South played in three diamonds doubled after West had opened one club and North had doubled. West began with the ace of clubs and was able to judge from the cards played that his partner held an even number of clubs – probably four.

At rubber bridge West continued with a second club. South ruffed and made the well-judged play of a low diamond, which West had to win with the singleton king. West switched to a heart now. Declarer won in dummy, took three rounds of spades, then crossed to dummy again and discarded his losing heart on a good spade. Thus he made the contract, losing just three diamonds and one club.

While the exact sequence of events could hardly be foreseen, the lead of the second club was pointless. It could only help the declarer. Instead, West should lead a heart at trick two, attacking dummy's entry. Now, if South plays three rounds of spades he runs into a ruff, and if he plays a diamond first, a second heart will remove dummy's last entry.

Second Test

Dealer South   Love all

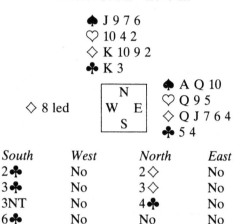

♠ J 9 7 6
♡ 10 4 2
◇ K 10 9 2
♣ K 3

◇ 8 led

N
W   E
S

♠ A Q 10
♡ Q 9 5
◇ Q J 7 6 4
♣ 5 4

South	West	North	East
2♣	No	2◇	No
3♣	No	3◇	No
3NT	No	4♣	No
6♣	No	No	No

North's four clubs was well judged, because the bidding could still stop in 4NT. South had other ideas, however.

West's lead of the 8 of diamonds ran to the 9, jack and ace. South played ace and another club, on which West played the 6 and 2, then led a spade from dummy. Sitting East, what is your general plan now?

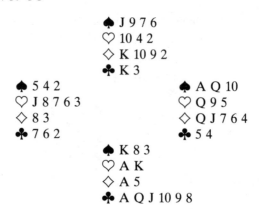

After some optimistic bidding South finishes in six clubs. West leads the 8 of diamonds through a suit bid by dummy, and this is covered by the 9, jack and ace. South plays ace and another club, West playing high-low, then leads a spade from dummy.

At the table East played a semi-deceptive queen of spades, but this did not save him from an eventual throw-in. South won with the king and played off his trumps, reducing East to one spade and two diamonds.

Nor does it help East to win with the ace of spades and exit in hearts. Again South plays off his winners and now East is squeezed in spades and diamonds.

Especially as partner has played high-low in trumps, showing three, East must win with the ace of spades and return a *diamond*. This kills the squeeze.

There was a hand on this general theme earlier in the book, so you can check to see whether you are improving!

54   Shock Treatment

Dealer South   Love all

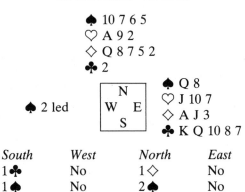

♠ 10 7 6 5
♡ A 9 2
◇ Q 8 7 5 2
♣ 2

♠ 2 led

♠ Q 8
♡ J 10 7
◇ A J 3
♣ K Q 10 8 7

South	West	North	East
1♣	No	1◇	No
1♠	No	2♠	No
4♠	No	No	No

Your partner, displaying unusual perception, leads a trump and your queen is headed by the ace. South leads the 9 of diamonds, 6 from West, 2 from North, and you win with the jack. You think for a moment about the jack of hearts, but decide that a second trump cannot be wrong.

The contract is made, nevertheless, and surprise, surprise! You get the blame. Why is that?

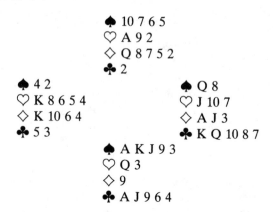

♠ 10 7 6 5
♡ A 9 2
◇ Q 8 7 5 2
♣ 2

♠ 4 2   ♠ Q 8
♡ K 8 6 5 4   ♡ J 10 7
◇ K 10 6 4   ◇ A J 3
♣ 5 3   ♣ K Q 10 8 7

♠ A K J 9 3
♡ Q 3
◇ 9
♣ A J 9 6 4

South, who has opened one club, plays in four spades. A low trump goes to the queen and ace, a diamond runs to the jack, and you return a second spade. Dummy wins with the 10 and has enough entries to establish the long diamond. He makes ten tricks by way of five spades, one heart, one diamond, one club, and two ruffs.

It's a shock to see partner looking reproachful. 'Did you have to play the queen of spades on the first trick?' he asks. 'You gave dummy the extra entry. If you play a low spade he can't get the long diamond going.'

Slight Flaw

Dealer North   N–S vulnerable

♠ A 9 7 6
♡ —
♢ K Q 8 7 6
♣ Q J 10 9

♠ K Q J 10
♡ 7 6 5 4
♢ 10 5
♣ 5 3 2

```
    N
 W     E
    S
```

South	West	North	East
—	—	1♢	No
2♡	No	2♠	No
3♣	No	4♣	No
4NT	No	5♢	No
5NT	No	6♢	No
6NT	No	No	No

You lead the king of spades, dummy plays low, East the 4 and declarer the 2.

At the table you might think: South has pushed his partner all the way from one diamond to 6NT. He has even invited a grand slam, by bidding 5NT. He is sure to hold top hearts, ace of diamonds, and probably A K of clubs. If his diamonds are A x x, he will surely have enough tricks. Is there any reason why I shouldn't lead a second spade? He can always play the ace of spades himself.

There is just one slight flaw in this analysis. Can you see what it is?

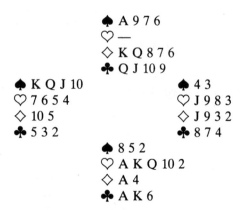

♠ A 9 7 6
♡ —
♢ K Q 8 7 6
♣ Q J 10 9

♠ K Q J 10
♡ 7 6 5 4
♢ 10 5
♣ 5 3 2

♠ 4 3
♡ J 9 8 3
♢ J 9 3 2
♣ 8 7 4

♠ 8 5 2
♡ A K Q 10 2
♢ A 4
♣ A K 6

West should look at it this way:

We are going to beat this slam only if my partner has protecting cards in hearts and diamonds. Even then, is there not a danger that he will be squeezed?

If West leads a second spade, South will win in dummy, run four clubs, cross to the ace of diamonds, and play off the top hearts. East, meanwhile, will be unable to keep his guard in both red suits.

It should not be too difficult to see that the awkward lead for South will be an early diamond. His problem, in technical terms, will be that after playing the squeeze card – the fourth club – he will have no entry to his own hand.

If you found the diamond lead at trick two, South will be left with the melancholy reflection that thirteen tricks in clubs would have been easy against any defence; not so easy to reach, however.

56   Small Trap

Dealer West   Game all

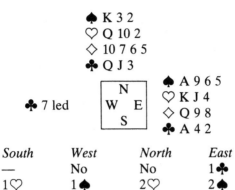

♠ K 3 2
♡ Q 10 2
◇ 10 7 6 5
♣ Q J 3

♠ A 9 6 5
♡ K J 4
◇ Q 9 8
♣ A 4 2

♣ 7 led

South	West	North	East
—	No	No	1♣
1♡	1♠	2♡	2♠
3♡	No	No	No

Playing a strong notrump when vulnerable, you open one club on the East hand. South buys the contract in three hearts and your partner leads a club to the jack and ace. You return a club, won by dummy's queen, and declarer leads the queen of hearts from the table. This can be a trap if partner holds a singleton ace, but that is not likely here, so you cover with the king. A second round runs to the 9, 10 and jack.

You have a fair picture of the South hand. His clubs are presumably K 10 9 8. Still, you have to be careful. What will you do next?

Answer 56

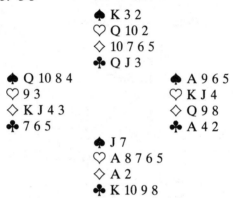

♠ K 3 2
♡ Q 10 2
◇ 10 7 6 5
♣ Q J 3

♠ Q 10 8 4
♡ 9 3
◇ K J 4 3
♣ 7 6 5

♠ A 9 6 5
♡ K J 4
◇ Q 9 8
♣ A 4 2

♠ J 7
♡ A 8 7 6 5
◇ A 2
♣ K 10 9 8

South plays in three hearts after East has opened one club. West leads a club to the ace and you return a club. The queen of hearts is covered and you win the next round with the jack.

It may seem safe and natural to exit with either a club or a heart, but see where that leads a few tricks later:

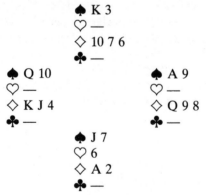

♠ K 3
♡ —
◇ 10 7 6
♣ —

♠ Q 10
♡ —
◇ K J 4
♣ —

♠ A 9
♡ —
◇ Q 9 8
♣ —

♠ J 7
♡ 6
◇ A 2
♣ —

On ♡ 6 everyone discards a diamond. Now ace and another diamond forces the defenders to open up the spades.

To avoid this trap, East must lead a diamond when in with the jack of hearts. The ending is difficult to foresee, but in general it is right to dislodge high cards.

57 Something Special

Dealer East   E–W vulnerable

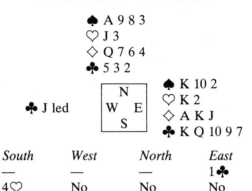

♠ A 9 8 3
♡ J 3
◇ Q 7 6 4
♣ 5 3 2

♣ J led

N
W   E
S

♠ K 10 2
♡ K 2
◇ A K J
♣ K Q 10 9 7

South	West	North	East
—	—	—	1♣
4♡	No	No	No

You cover the jack of clubs with the queen, but South wins and leads the queen of spades, on which partner plays the 4 and dummy the 3. Do you see a good plan for the defence?

Answer 57

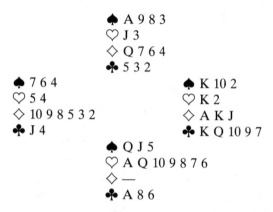

♠ A 9 8 3
♡ J 3
♢ Q 7 6 4
♣ 5 3 2

♠ 7 6 4
♡ 5 4
♢ 10 9 8 5 3 2
♣ J 4

♠ K 10 2
♡ K 2
♢ A K J
♣ K Q 10 9 7

♠ Q J 5
♡ A Q 10 9 8 7 6
♢ —
♣ A 8 6

East opens one club and South overcalls with four hearts. You are tempted to double, but the extra 50 may not be worth much, and furthermore, are you sure you play as well as Zia Mahmood, who held the East cards?

West led the jack of clubs. South won and ran the queen of spades. Since partner would not have led the jack from J x x, you can be sure of three tricks – two in clubs and one in spades. However, South won't have a losing diamond as well.

Something special is needed, and Zia found it: on the queen of spades he dropped the 10. The declarer thought: If that's a singleton it would be dangerous for me to cross to dummy for the heart finesse. East will ruff, give partner the lead on the second or third round of clubs, and ruff another spade. I had better play ace and another heart.

Following this play, he lost four tricks when Zia turned up with the king of spades.

Special Gift

Dealer North   Love all

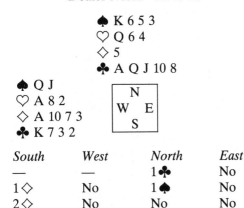

♠ K 6 5 3
♡ Q 6 4
◇ 5
♣ A Q J 10 8

♠ Q J
♡ A 8 2
◇ A 10 7 3
♣ K 7 3 2

South	West	North	East
—	—	1♣	No
1◇	No	1♠	No
2◇	No	No	No

West leads the queen of spades and follows with the jack, which also holds. South has followed with the 9 and 10, so it looks as though partner has five to the ace.

At trick three you try the 7 of clubs. Dummy's queen wins, East playing the 6 and declarer the 4.

South leads a diamond from the table: 5, 2, Q, A. You can see five tricks for the defence. Where will the sixth come from? Partner may possibly hold one of the red kings, but you don't want to rely on this.

Answer 58

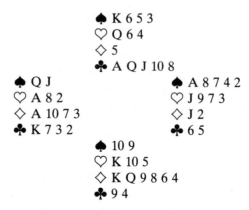

♠ K 6 5 3
♡ Q 6 4
♢ 5
♣ A Q J 10 8

♠ Q J
♡ A 8 2
♢ A 10 7 3
♣ K 7 3 2

♠ A 8 7 4 2
♡ J 9 7 3
♢ J 2
♣ 6 5

♠ 10 9
♡ K 10 5
♢ K Q 9 8 6 4
♣ 9 4

South plays in two diamonds and you win the first two tricks with the queen and jack of spades. You try the 7 of clubs; queen from dummy, 6 from East, 4 from South. Then a diamond from the table runs to the queen and ace.

You have made two tricks in spades, are sure of at least two in diamonds, and the ace of hearts won't run away. Since partner would not have played the 6 of clubs from 9 6 5, you can be fairly sure that the clubs are 2–2.

Has the idea struck you now? Lead the king of clubs, forcing dummy to win. Now, if partner has either the 9 or jack of diamonds you will surely promote an extra winner in the trump suit. For example, if declarer leads a heart to the 10 and ace, you lead a third club and partner's jack of diamonds will ensure two tricks for your ◇ 10 7 3. A neat coup to bring off at the table!

59   The Reason Why

Dealer South   Game all

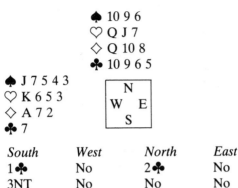

♠ 10 9 6
♡ Q J 7
◇ Q 10 8
♣ 10 9 6 5

♠ J 7 5 4 3
♡ K 6 5 3
◇ A 7 2
♣ 7

South	West	North	East
1♣	No	2♣	No
3NT	No	No	No

Many players would have responded one diamond on the North hand, but one advantage of two clubs was that this made it more difficult for East to intervene.

West led a low spade, which ran to the king and ace. After some thought the declarer played ace and another heart. West won with the king, while his partner played the 8 followed by the 4.

West pondered for some while before finding the best continuation. What was it?

Answer 59

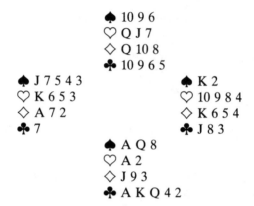

♠ 10 9 6
♥ Q J 7
♦ Q 10 8
♣ 10 9 6 5

♠ J 7 5 4 3
♥ K 6 5 3
♦ A 7 2
♣ 7

♠ K 2
♥ 10 9 8 4
♦ K 6 5 4
♣ J 8 3

♠ A Q 8
♥ A 2
♦ J 9 3
♣ A K Q 4 2

South might have opened 2NT, but he preferred one club and went to 3NT over his partner's raise to two clubs. West led a low spade, which was covered by the king and ace.

The difficulty with this sort of hand is that the clubs may be blocked. If South has to win the fourth round in dummy and take the heart finesse, the situation will be clear to the defenders: West will lead a low diamond and a spade will come back.

South made the defence more difficult by beginning with ace and another heart. West won and his partner echoed with the 8 and the 4, clearly showing length.

It is often difficult to realize that declarer's main suit is blocked, but West worked out here what was happening. South had to have some reason for playing on a suit in which he was comparatively short. West found a switch to a low diamond, a spade came back, and South could run only eight tricks.

60   The Wind Blows

Dealer East   N–S vulnerable

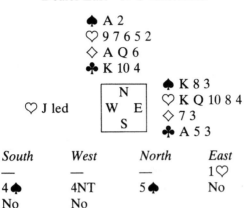

♠ A 2
♡ 9 7 6 5 2
◇ A Q 6
♣ K 10 4

♡ J led

♠ K 8 3
♡ K Q 10 8 4
◇ 7 3
♣ A 5 3

South	West	North	East
—	—	—	1♡
4♠	4NT	5♠	No
No	No		

Your partner in a pairs event is a player of somewhat erratic habits and at first you are not sure what his 4NT was intended to convey. When you see the dummy you realize that he holds a minor two-suiter.

You overtake the jack of hearts and South wins with the ace. After some consideration he plays a diamond to the queen, cashes the ace, and leads a third round from the table.

Have you decided which way the wind is blowing?

Answer 60

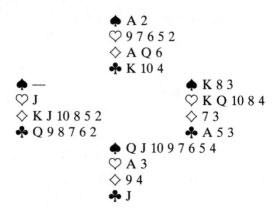

```
              ♠ A 2
              ♡ 9 7 6 5 2
              ◇ A Q 6
              ♣ K 10 4
♠ —                        ♠ K 8 3
♡ J                        ♡ K Q 10 8 4
◇ K J 10 8 5 2             ◇ 7 3
♣ Q 9 8 7 6 2             ♣ A 5 3
              ♠ Q J 10 9 7 6 5 4
              ♡ A 3
              ◇ 9 4
              ♣ J
```

South plays in five spades after you have opened one heart and West has bid 4NT to indicate length in the minors.

The jack of hearts is covered by the queen and ace. South finesses the queen of diamonds, cashes the ace, and leads a third round from dummy.

South has played cleverly. He intends on this trick to discard the jack of clubs. When West wins he will be on play: a diamond will be ruffed by the ace of spades, South discarding his heart loser, and a club will be covered by the 10 and ace, South ruffing. Then his losing heart will go away on the king of clubs.

A neat example of the *Scissors coup*; but you can save your side by inserting a low trump when the third diamond is led.

61

Through the Slips

Dealer West   Love all

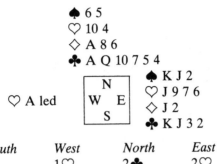

```
              ♠ 6 5
              ♡ 10 4
              ◇ A 8 6
              ♣ A Q 10 7 5 4
                                ♠ K J 2
                    N           ♡ J 9 7 6
    ♡ A led      W     E        ◇ J 2
                    S           ♣ K J 3 2
```

South	West	North	East
—	1♡	2♣	2♡
3♠	No	4♠	dble
No	No	No	

West cashed ace and king of hearts, then switched to the 5 of diamonds. South won in dummy and led a low trump from the table. Sitting East, what is your defensive plan?

Answer 61

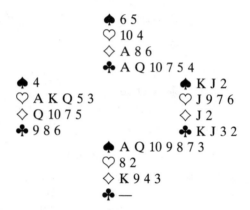

```
              ♠ 6 5
              ♡ 10 4
              ◇ A 8 6
              ♣ A Q 10 7 5 4
♠ 4                              ♠ K J 2
♡ A K Q 5 3                      ♡ J 9 7 6
◇ Q 10 7 5                       ◇ J 2
♣ 9 8 6                          ♣ K J 3 2
              ♠ A Q 10 9 8 7 3
              ♡ 8 2
              ◇ K 9 4 3
              ♣ —
```

After West had opened one heart and North had overcalled in clubs, South jumped to three spades and North raised to game. This was doubled by East, and the defence began with two top hearts, followed by a low diamond. Declarer won in dummy and advanced the 5 of spades.

East's 2 of spades was on the table before he had given the situation a moment's thought. Reflecting that East would not have doubled four spades unless he had a probable trump trick, South let the 5 run. Then a diamond was thrown on the ace of clubs and only a diamond was lost.

It was clever play by the declarer to lead a trump without cashing the ace of clubs. There may be no logical reason for East to make a mistake as the play went, but if the ace of clubs had been cashed he would have realized that the defence would need to take a trump and a diamond.

62

Too Confident

Dealer South   Love all

```
              ♠ 6 4
              ♡ A K 8 4 2
              ◇ A 2
              ♣ 10 8 7 5
  ♠ K Q 9 2    ┌─────────┐
  ♡ 10 3       │    N    │
  ◇ J 8 6      │  W   E  │
  ♣ K J 6 2    │    S    │
              └─────────┘
```

South	West	North	East
1♠	No	2♡	No
2♠	No	3♣	No
3◇	No	3♠	No
4♠	No	No	No

Since North pondered for a while before bidding three clubs you decide that he is not strong in the suit and you lead the 2 of clubs. Partner wins with the ace and declarer drops the queen. East has the wit to return a trump, South plays the jack and you win with the queen.

How do you plan to defend from this point?

Answer 62

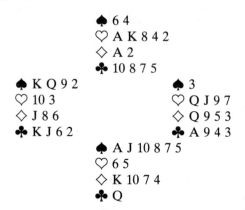

```
              ♠ 6 4
              ♡ A K 8 4 2
              ◇ A 2
              ♣ 10 8 7 5
♠ K Q 9 2                    ♠ 3
♡ 10 3                       ♡ Q J 9 7
◇ J 8 6                      ◇ Q 9 5 3
♣ K J 6 2                    ♣ A 9 4 3
              ♠ A J 10 8 7 5
              ♡ 6 5
              ◇ K 10 7 4
              ♣ Q
```

South plays in four spades after a sequence that has marked him with six spades and four diamonds. You lead the 2 of clubs to partner's ace and East returns a spade, which is covered by the jack and queen.

At this point you may conclude that you have two trump tricks still to come, and you may think of exiting in one of the side suits. However, you may be disillusioned. If he believes your lead of the 2 of clubs – and especially if you thought for a moment about doubling four spades – South may ruff the third diamond and make five tricks with three club ruffs and two hearts. When he exits with his fourth diamond you will be obliged to ruff and lead into the spade tenace.

It can hardly be wrong to save a diamond trick by exiting with a trump when in with the queen of spades. Now South will need to play well (taking three club ruffs in hand) to avoid going two down.

63   **Well Timed Offer**

Dealer South   Love all

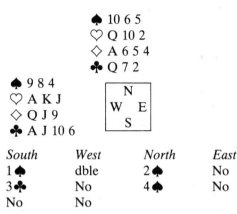

        ♠ 10 6 5
        ♡ Q 10 2
        ◇ A 6 5 4
        ♣ Q 7 2

♠ 9 8 4
♡ A K J
◇ Q J 9
♣ A J 10 6

South	West	North	East
1♠	dble	2♠	No
3♣	No	4♠	No
No	No		

North–South are playing five-card majors and North is entitled to bid the game after South's invitation.

On your lead of the ace of hearts partner plays the 4 and declarer the 7. At this point you cannot be sure of the heart distribution. Not wanting to give anything away, you switch to a trump. South wins and plays a second heart. You win with the king and partner plays the 5. What is the best line now?

Answer 63

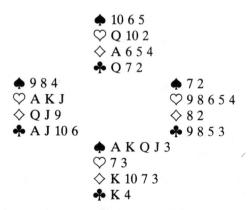

♠ 10 6 5
♡ Q 10 2
◇ A 6 5 4
♣ Q 7 2

♠ 9 8 4
♡ A K J
◇ Q J 9
♣ A J 10 6

♠ 7 2
♡ 9 8 6 5 4
◇ 8 2
♣ 9 8 5 3

♠ A K Q J 3
♡ 7 3
◇ K 10 7 3
♣ K 4

Defending against four spades, you lead the ace of hearts and switch to a trump. South wins and leads a second heart, which you win.

You have a picture of the heart situation now and it seems reasonably safe to lead the queen of diamonds or a second trump. It may not be easy to foresee, but there is a danger in this neutral play. South will draw trumps and lead a low club from hand. Now you will be on the horns of the proverbial dilemma. If you let dummy's queen win, South will discard the king of clubs on the queen of hearts; and if you win with the ace of clubs, you will be establishing two diamond discards.

The best play in such situations, when you *know* that the queen of hearts is going to provide a discard, is to lead the third heart. Then it is South who will be looking for a useful discard.

64   Why the Duck?

Dealer South   Game all

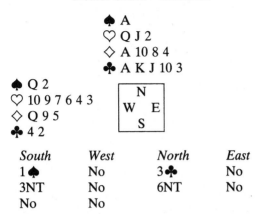

♠ A
♡ Q J 2
◇ A 10 8 4
♣ A K J 10 3

♠ Q 2
♡ 10 9 7 6 4 3
◇ Q 9 5
♣ 4 2

South	West	North	East
1♠	No	3♣	No
3NT	No	6NT	No
No	No		

Enquiry reveals that South's 3NT rebid, over the force, is likely to show a minimum, not a medium hand as in some systems.

Your lead of the 10 of hearts is covered by the jack, king and ace. Declarer leads a spade to the ace, returns to the queen of clubs, and then leads a low spade, so you find yourself on lead.

Taking things in turn, why has declarer given up this trick in spades? Is it safe to play another heart? Does any other play look better?

Answer 64

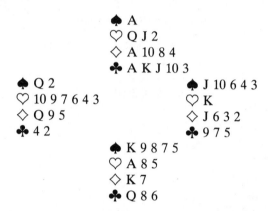

```
              ♠ A
              ♡ Q J 2
              ◇ A 10 8 4
              ♣ A K J 10 3
♠ Q 2                         ♠ J 10 6 4 3
♡ 10 9 7 6 4 3                ♡ K
◇ Q 9 5                       ◇ J 6 3 2
♣ 4 2                         ♣ 9 7 5
              ♠ K 9 8 7 5
              ♡ A 8 5
              ◇ K 7
              ♣ Q 8 6
```

South opens one spade and finishes in 6NT. You lead the 10 of hearts and after some thought the declarer takes the wrong view, playing the jack from dummy. He wins the king with the ace, crosses to the ace of spades, and returns to the queen of clubs. Then he leads the 7 of spades and you are in with the queen.

It is clear that he has given up the trick in spades because he is preparing for a possible squeeze. You can see where eleven tricks are coming from: two spades, two hearts, two diamonds, and five clubs. If South had held the jack of diamonds he would have established a twelfth trick by giving up a diamond, so you can place your partner with the jack of diamonds and also the jack of spades (for otherwise this would be the declarer's twelfth trick).

To lead the 9 of hearts would achieve nothing even if it pinned the 8. You must attack diamonds, and the card to play is the queen. South wins with the king, but no squeeze is possible because you command the hearts and your partner the diamonds. It is true that partner will also have the guard in spades, but after running the clubs South will have no entry to his own hand.

Idiot's Delight

Dealer East   N–S vulnerable

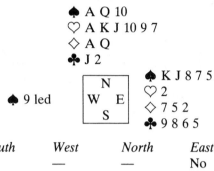

```
              ♠ A Q 10
              ♡ A K J 10 9 7
              ◇ A Q
              ♣ J 2
                              ♠ K J 8 7 5
                              ♡ 2
    ♠ 9 led                   ◇ 7 5 2
                              ♣ 9 8 6 5
```

South	West	North	East
—	—	—	No
No	1◇	2◇	No
2♡	No	4♡	No
No	No		

Declarer tries the queen of spades from dummy and you win with the king. You may assume that South is not one of those idiots who would bid two hearts with three small and a bad hand, so you must hope to make two spades and two clubs. It may not be quite so easy as you think.

Answer 65

                ♠ A Q 10
                ♡ A K J 10 9 7
                ◇ A Q
                ♣ J 2

♠ 9 4   ♠ K J 8 7 5
♡ 8 3   ♡ 2
◇ K J 10 9 4   ◇ 7 5 2
♣ A Q 10 7   ♣ 9 8 6 5

                ♠ 6 3 2
                ♡ Q 6 5 4
                ◇ 8 6 3
                ♣ K 4 3

South plays in four hearts after West has opened one diamond in third position and North has forced with two diamonds. West leads the 9 of spades and South puts in the queen, which you win with the king.

Now you have a problem, though it may not seem so at the time. If you make the obvious return of a club, West will win and lead another spade. South will take with the ace, draw two rounds of trumps, then run the jack of clubs to West's ace. The 10 of spades will go away on the king of clubs and South will make the remainder.

When you win the first trick with the king of spades you must realize that a club return can only serve to set up a trick for the declarer. The winning play is the singleton trump. Say that declarer draws the second trump, cashes the ace of spades, and exits with the jack of clubs. West leads a diamond now, and South cannot avoid the loss of two spades and two clubs. Well done, you have won the Brilliancy Prize by leading a singleton 2!